THE LIFE AND DEATH
OF HANGMAN THOMAS

J. M. Q. DAVIES attended Greek schools during his childhood in Thessaloniki and read Modern Greek and German at Oxford before pursuing an academic career in English and Comparative Literature, teaching at the Universities of California, Alberta, Melbourne, Darwin and Waseda. He is the author of a monograph, *Blake's Milton designs: the dynamics of meaning* (1993), has edited a collection of essays, *Bridging the gap: literary theory in the classroom* (1994), and written articles on modern fiction, literary theory, fantasy and new literatures in English. His translations from German and Modern Greek are:

*German tales of fantasy, horror and the grotesque* (Longman Cheshire, 1987)

ARTHUR SCHNITZLER, *Selected short fiction* (Angel Classics, 1999) — *Dream story* (Penguin, 1999) — *Round dance and other plays* (Oxford World's Classics, 2004)

THOMAS SCHIPPERGES, *Prokofiev* (Haus, 2003)

HUGO VON HOFMANNSTHAL, *Selected tales* (Angel Classics, 2007)

KONSTANTINOS THEOTOKIS, *Slaves in their chains* (Angel Classics, 2014)

OTHER TRANSLATIONS OF GREEK LITERATURE
FROM COLENSO BOOKS

*Sweet-voiced Sappho*, verse translations from SAPPHO and other Ancient Greek poets by Theodore Stephanides (2015)

IAKOVOS KAMBANELLIS, *Three plays (The courtyard of wonders, The four legs of the table, Ibsenland)* translated by Marjorie Chambers (2015)

KONSTANTINOS THEOTOKIS, *Corfiot tales*, translated by J. M. Q. Davies (expected 2017)

# THE LIFE AND DEATH

## OF

# HANGMAN THOMAS

*by*

KONSTANTINOS THEOTOKIS

*translated from the Greek
with an Introduction and Notes*

*by*

J. M. Q. DAVIES

COLENSO BOOKS
2016

This translation first published September 2016 by
Colenso Books
68 Palatine Road, London N16 8ST, UK
colensobooks@gmail.com

Reprinted with minor corrections January 2017
and December 2017

ISBN 978-0-9928632-4-1

First published 1920 as
Ἡ ζωὴ καὶ ὁ θάνατος τοῦ Καραβέλα
by Οἶκος Γ. Ι. Βασιλείου, Athens.

Translation, Introduction and Notes copyright © 2016 J. M. Q. Davies

The image on the front cover is *Europa and the Bull*, 1951–52 (earthenware, coloured slips & clear glaze) by Arthur Boyd (1920–1999). Arthur Boyd Gift 1975 to the National Gallery of Australia. Copyright © National Gallery of Australia, Canberra. Reproduced with permission of the National Gallery of Australia and Bridgeman Images, London.

Printed and bound in Great Britain by
Lightning Source UK Ltd
Chapter House, Pitfield, Kiln Farm,
Milton Keynes MK11 3LW, UK

# CONTENTS

| | |
|---|---|
| Introduction | vii |
|    Corfu — the historical background | vii |
|    Konstantinos Theotokis (1872–1923) — his life and works | x |
|    *The life and death of Hangman Thomas* (1920) | xiv |
|    A note on the translation | xvii |
| The Life and Death of Hangman Thomas | 1 |
|    Chapter I | 3 |
|    Chapter II | 15 |
|    Chapter III | 26 |
|    Chapter IV | 36 |
|    Chapter V | 43 |
|    Chapter VI | 54 |
|    Chapter VII | 61 |
|    Chapter VIII | 69 |
|    Chapter IX | 76 |
|    Chapter X | 85 |
|    Chapter XI | 95 |
|    Chapter XII | 107 |
|    Chapter XIII | 113 |
| Notes | 123 |
| Bibliography | 130 |

# INTRODUCTION

## CORFU — THE HISTORICAL BACKGROUND

There is a romantic aura to the history of cosmopolitan Corfu and the Ionian Islands, with their Homeric ghosts, Byzantine forts, Venetian mansions, French arcades and British palaces, which all but eclipses the lives of their indigenous Greek peasantry. Part of the Byzantine empire for nearly a thousand years, they were acquired first by the Normans then by the Venetians, who in 1386 purchased Corfu as a command centre for their maritime affairs, strengthening its fort to keep the Turks at bay and establishing an Italianized Greek aristocracy to oversee production of the all-important cash crops — olives on Corfu and currants bound for Britain on Cephalonia and Zante. Some of these ruling families had fled from Constantinople after its capitulation to the Turks in 1453, and included merchants, buccaneers and politicians, but also theologians, scholars and translators who helped to preserve Greece's cultural heritage and provide a beacon for the mainland Greeks under the Ottoman yoke. Venice, nominally Catholic, took a pragmatic approach toward religion on Corfu, accepting the Orthodox Patriarch's authority and admitting Jewish refugees from the Spanish Inquisition. But it neglected public education, and higher professional training could only be obtained abroad. And despite Corfu's natural fertility, the peasants' lives were far from idyllic, as they had to return up to half of their proceeds to the landlord and were ministered to by often ill-educated clergy dependent on fees for rites and inclined to exploit their charges' superstitions.[1] Moreover as cultural life in town improved, with carnivals, opera and theatre, many landlords absented themselves from their *archondika*, or country houses, while inadequate law enforcement in the villages encouraged personal vendettas.

More liberal winds of change swept through the Ionian Islands during the Romantic era, when successive victorious Powers occupied

---

[1] Gallant (*Modern Greece*, 94f) highlights differences between tenant farming and sharecropping under the Ionian feudal system and elsewhere in Greece.

and attempted to reform them. Having taken over Venice in 1797, Napoleon dispatched troops to Corfu, regarding it as the key to the Adriatic, and the feudal system was declared abolished, the *Libro d'Oro* (the honour roll of the Venetian nobles) burned and republican 'trees of liberty' raised in village squares. After the Battle of the Nile, the French were ousted by a coalition of the Russians and the Turks (traditionally bitter rivals in the Balkans), who set up a semi-independent Heptanesian Republic under the protection of the Tzar and paying tribute to the Porte. But the French returned in 1807 and stayed long enough to bring a touch of Parisian culture to Corfu, founding an arcade modelled on the Rue de Rivoli, an Ionian Society and several liberal periodicals. In 1815 after Napoleon's defeat the Ionian Islands became a British Protectorate, ruled by a succession of colourful Lord High Commissioners, assisted by a senate drawn from the old Italianized noble families (Theotokis, Metaxas, Flamburiari), a legislative assembly and a constitution.

When the Greek War of Independence against the Ottomans broke out in 1821, there was considerable enthusiasm among the islanders, who, despite centuries of Venetian rule, identified themselves as Orthodox and Greek. Indeed, with Athens as yet little more than a market town, a mosque still nestling against the Parthenon, it did not seem impossible that Corfu might become the capital of a liberated modern Greece. But in compliance with Britain's treaty obligations to the Turks, the first Lord High Commissioner, Sir Thomas Maitland, insisted that the Ionian Islands remain strictly neutral and hanged or imprisoned local Greek freedom fighters and agitators from the *Philiki Eteria*, the secret society started in Odessa. Even so, when the struggle between Turks and rival Greek warlords on the mainland reached a stalemate, it was the Corfiot Count John Capodistrias who in 1827 was accepted by the Powers to head a fledgling Greek nation — only to be assassinated in 1831 and replaced by the Bavarian Otto as King of the Hellenes. And it was the Zantean romantic poet Count Dionysios Solomos whose 'Hymn to Liberty' in ballad stanzas and demotic Greek would provide the national anthem.

Maitland's other measures were more progressive. He ended the custom of confining the Jews to the ghetto at night, legislated to curb the nobles' exploitation of the peasants and initiated a programme of building roads, bridges, schools and prisons which helped to revive the economy, increase law and order and reduce the isolation of the villages. It was also early in the Protectorate that the eccentric philhellene, Lord Guilford — whose fondness for dressing up like Plato reflected a widespread assumption that the Greeks and their language had remained unchanged since Classical Antiquity — spent his fortune on establishing the Ionian Academy, the first modern Greek institute of higher learning. In mid-century another eccentric, Edward Lear, who did learn some modern Greek and admired the local folk costumes and dances, painted and later published a series of picturesque landscapes of the Ionian Islands. All of these civilizing measures, however, retarded rather than extinguishing support for union with the mainland and the *Megali Idea*, the grand irredentist idea of reuniting the Greeks of Thessaly, Macedonia, Crete, Asia Minor and all the islands within a new Byzantium. And when the reign of the autocratic and unpopular King Otto ended in 1864, the British finally ceded the Ionian Islands to Greece in return for securing their candidate, the Danish-born King George I, on the Greek throne.

When the British left, spectacularly blowing up parts of the fortifications, the world of residency balls, dinners, hunts and picnics ended and the nobility retired to their estates or sought posts in more egalitarian Athens. But Corfu's romantic aura lingered and by the *Belle Epoque* it had become a retreat for Europe's high society, the Greek royals using the Palace of St Michael and St George, the neurotic Habsburg empress Elizabeth visiting her sea-view 'Achilleon', the Kaiser building a private jetty for his yachts and motorcars, and scholars and archaeologists like Heinrich Schliemann, 'lured by the siren voices of Homeric geography', exploring Cephalonia, Ithaca, and Lefkas.[2] During the First World War Corfu briefly became a refugee camp for the Serbian army, driven west by the Bulgarians in the scramble for Ottoman territory (Greece and Serbia were at that point allies). A glimpse of Corfu in the years before the Axis bombings of 1943 as an enchanted isle of cypresses and sapphire bays, peopled by reclusive Counts, savant doctors and exotic locals watching shadow-puppet plays, is provided by Lawrence Durrell in his *Prospero's Cell*.

---

[2] Young (*Corfu and the other Ionian Islands*, 94) summarizes the archeological quest for Homeric sites in an excellent account of the Islands' sociopolitical and cultural history.

INTRODUCTION

## KONSTANTINOS THEOTOKIS (1872–1923)
## HIS LIFE AND WORKS

Konstantinos Theotokis, after Solomos the Ionian Islands' most distinguished writer and one of Greece's more intriguing men of letters, was steeped in these historical and cultural traditions by virtue of his birth. An idealistic nobleman turned socialist, who like Tolstoy forfeited his feudal patrimony, he matured artistically on the very cusp of Modernism and, working principally in the *Verismo*, or Naturalist mode of Giovanni Verga (1840–1922) and Émile Zola (1840–1902), he paid tribute to the harsh unrecorded lives of the Greek peasantry in short stories and novellas of immense dramatic power and insight. And in his crowning satiric novel, *Slaves in their chains* (1922), which chronicles the decline of a Corfiot noble family unable to compete in the encroaching capitalist world, he used his insider's knowledge to expose the corruptness and decadence of the island's social elite before the First World War. Corfu is almost never actually named in any of these works, however, doubtless so as not to obscure their more universal relevance.

Theotokis's family had migrated to Corfu and Crete after the fall of Constantinople and been ennobled by the Venetians during the seventeenth century, and he could lay claim to such illustrious figures as the painter Dominikos Theotokopoulos (El Greco), Emmanouil Theotokis, first president of the Ionian Senate under the British, and George Theotokis, thrice prime minister of Greece, among his extended clan. His father, Count Markos Theotokis, a Corfiot archivist and scholar given to dwelling on the family's former glories, was typical of his class in regarding the French Revolution and bourgeois democracy as inventions of the Jews and Masons. In his forties, no heir being forthcoming from his bachelor elder brother Alexandros, Markos married the beautiful and musical seventeen-year-old Angeliki Polyla (also from a patrician family and niece of Iakovos Polylas, editor of Solomos's posthumous papers) and sired ten children. Dinos, as their first son was affectionately called, excelled in maths and science at school and enjoyed amateur theatricals and writing playlets, aptitudes later reflected in the formal precision and dramatic structure of his fiction. But as a student in Paris he fell in with the city's *jeunesse dorée*, flaunting his titled status, squandering a fortune sent by his doting uncle (permanently impoverishing his siblings) and leaving for Venice without taking a degree. There, still only nineteen, he fell in love with and proposed to Ernestine von Malowitz, a convent-bred Catholic Bohemian baroness almost as old as his own mother. Summoned to Venice to the rescue, Count Markos warned her of his son's temperamental nature and modest expectations, but she insisted that her young suitor was honour bound, and after waiting until Dinos's majority the couple married in Prague and settled on the Theotokis ramshackle *archondiko* outside the village of Karousades in the north of Corfu opposite Albania.

Here Theotokis prepared for the cultural leadership role he felt expected of him by embarking on an ambitious programme of self-education, reading extensively in European literature and philosophy, particularly Nietzsche, Schopenhauer and, later, Marx; teaching himself Sanskrit; and on occasion using his scientific knowledge to assist his peasants and their livestock with their ailments. Over the ensuing decades, in addition to producing the outstanding realistic fiction for which he is chiefly remembered, he translated extensively from Lucretius, the Indian classics, Shakespeare, Goethe, Heine, Flaubert, Turgenev and Bertrand Russell, continuing Corfu's longstanding tradition of keeping Ottoman-held Greece abreast of western thought. His early experiments with fiction included a bandit novel, *Vie de montagne* (1895), written in French, a Nietzschean rhapsody entitled *Passion* (1899), and short exotic allegories influenced by Symbolism and Aestheticism such as 'Satni's dream' or the apocalyptic 'Waning of the world'. Important in helping him decide to write in Greek was his friendship with the older poet, Sanskrit scholar and ardent nationalist, Lorentzos Mavilis, who would later die fighting in the First Balkan War. And it was under his sway that Theotokis, emulating his own heroic ancestors, took part in the insurrection against the Turks in Crete in 1896 and again in Thessaly in 1897. By the turn of the century he had begun to write his *Corfiot tales*, published originally in demotic journals like *Techni* and *Noumas* and collected and published posthumously (in 1935) by his friend and co-editor on the journal *Corfiot Anthology* (*Kerkyraïka Antholoyia*), the poet Irene Dendrinou. Unlike many idyllic village sketches of the period, they are totally unsentimental and range from short horrific stories about honour killings like 'Face Down', or the psychologically tense 'Was it a Sin', exploring the dilemmas of a priest, to more extended studies such as 'Illicit Love', dealing with incest and the powerlessness of peasant women. Collectively they are a contribution to the sub-genre pioneered by writers like Alexandros Papadiamandis (1851–1911) and Andreas Karkavitsas (1866–1922) known as *ithographia*, which focused on fast vanishing regional customs and morality as a way of defining Greece's post-Ottoman identity.

Tragedy struck in 1900 when his only daughter died of meningitis at the age of five, after which he and Ernestine became increasingly estranged. Initially their marriage had been idyllic, but gradually Ernestine's village isolation and Dinos's violent temper and peccadillos with the peasant maidens took their toll. There had been furious rows — on one occasion when she returned from a shopping spree without his requests he flung her purchases into the fire — and, as divorce was out of the question for a Catholic, she sought consolation in religion — the novelist Nikos Kazantzakis' first wife Galatea called her a 'pious goose' — and he in his work. Much of all this would appear transmuted in his fiction, which contains several memorable portraits of passionate women and some of the most powerful scenes of lust and recrimination outside Tolstoy.

In 1907–08, during two semesters at Munich University, Theotokis became more seriously interested in Marxism as an alternative to the nationalism favoured by Mavilis, and on his return to Corfu he helped found a local socialist club. The extent of his alienation from his own caste by this point can be gauged from his refusal to accommodate the Kaiser's request for stage adaptations of his peasant stories. His most explicitly socialist and early feminist novel *Honour and cash* (1912) is set in Corfu's quayside suburb of Mandouki and involves the conflict between a middle-aged factory worker and her daughter's highborn seducer, who has taken to smuggling rather than stoop to honest labour and makes extortionate dowry demands. His next novel in order of publication, *The convict* (1919), is more psychological in emphasis, reflecting the influence of Dostoevsky, and focuses on a peasant 'innocent' falsely accused of murdering his master.[3] His most

---

[3] Because Theotokis's last three novels were all published towards the end of his life and their composition overlapped, it has been suggested that *The convict* with its Christian message may represent his final views and a partial retreat from his earlier optimism about revolutionary socialism.

humorous village novel, *The life and death of Hangman Thomas* (1920), is a dark tragicomedy of infatuation in old age which emphasizes the oppressive power of the collective. *Slaves in their chains* (1922), his longest and most personal work, is a tragicomic urban novel — pervaded, like Mann's *Buddenbrooks* (1901) or Galsworthy's *Forsyte Saga* (1922) by a very *fin-de-siècle* sense of doom — which dramatizes a local Corfiot family's descent into financial and moral bankruptcy, suicide and madness. With its extensive supporting cast of ambitious doctors, Jewish loan-sharks, ardent mistresses, student radicals, eccentric poetasters, unemployed *flâneurs* and nepotistic politicians, it provides a savagely satirical panorama of Corfu's *beau monde* in the years leading up to the First World War for which he was never quite forgiven locally. During the war, Theotokis's distrust of German imperialism caused him to side with the pro-Entente position of prime minister Eleftherios Venizelos in the national schism and against King Constantine, who was married to the Kaiser's sister and favoured Greek neutrality.

After the war, when his wife Ernestine had her Bohemian inheritance confiscated by the new Czech state, Theotokis was obliged for the first time in his life to seek gainful employment — as a civil servant in Athens. He lived just long enough to witness the demise of the *Megali Idea* with the humiliating rout of the Greek occupation forces in western Turkey by the nationalist leader Mustapha Kemal in 1922, and the ensuing massacre and expulsion of the Greek residents of Smyrna. In 1923 Theotokis succumbed to stomach cancer at the age of fifty-one, his wife taunting him that his suffering was a punishment from God for all the pain he had inflicted on her. To a friend he confided sadly that he felt he still had at least a decade's work left in him.

Theotokis only gradually achieved the posthumous recognition he deserved, partly because he was an outsider in Athenian literary circles, partly because as a regionalist he had less to offer urban middle class readers than novelists like Grigorios Xenopoulos or George Theotokas, whose realistic fiction mirrored their drab lives; while internationally he was eclipsed by the next generation of prose writers, pre-eminently Nikos Kazantzakis, but also Stratis Myrivilis and Ilias Venezis, whose novels about the First World War and the legacy of the Smyrna disaster had more immediate appeal for translators. But his use of demotic Greek in the liberal tradition of Solomos, as against the archaizing *katharevousa*, or 'purified' Greek favoured by the learned, which grafted ancient Greek forms onto the simpler post-Ottoman vernacular and was used in secondary schools and newspapers down to 1976, has meant that his work continues to be accessible to younger readers.[4]

## THE LIFE AND DEATH OF HANGMAN THOMAS (1920)

Formally Theotokis's most concise, symmetrical and perfect work of fiction, *The life and death of Hangman Thomas* returns to the themes and primal passions of the earlier *Corfiot tales*, but it explores them with much deeper sympathy and understanding and is altogether richer and subtler in tone and literary resonance. It is at once a tragicomedy of lust in old age, a study of vengeance and social alienation and a parable of modern materialist greed. As a realistic novel with echoes of Greek Tragedy it presents a Social-Darwinist world of relentless savagery, rivalling Verga's harshest Sicilian tales, or Karkavitsas's *The beggar* (1897), but filtered through Theotokis's reforming socialist conscience. At the same time it is deeply indebted to situation comedy and the characters of *opéra bouffe*; and its sordid Naturalist scenes are leavened by the sheer comedic exuberance and vitality of the characters, as they try to outfox, seduce and get back at one another. And the pace is quickened by Theotokis's skilful use of Verga's principle of *prosa dialogata*, events being dramatically presented through spicy dialogue in scenes as highly charged and tightly orchestrated as in a play by Molière. There are also Falstaffian parallels — particularly with Verdi's opera, *Falstaff* — and several slapstick moments in the Punch and Judy mode of Karaghiozis, the widely popular Greek shadow-puppet hero with his phallic arm.[5]

Thomas Kapsalis, an amorous irascible old peasant nicknamed the 'hangman' and saddled with a dying wife, lives next door to the Statiris brothers, and the main plot revolves round his infatuation with the younger brother Yannis's attractive wife Maria, and the elder brother

---

[4] For a full discussion of the so-called 'language issue' and its sociopolitical and literary ramifications, see Beaton, *An Introduction to modern Greek literature*, 296f; and Mackridge, *Language and national identity in Greece* and 'Venise après Venise'.
[5] See Lawrence Durrell, 'Karaghiosis: the laic hero' (*Prospero's Cell*, 44-57).

Argyris's schemes to acquire his house. This situation is mirrored in the subplot involving Maria's father, the local notary, who is being dispossessed by Maria's sister and her husband, the village priest. The Statiris brothers too are deftly counterpointed, as are their respective wives, the family tensions reflecting class relations in the world at large. The fat consumptive Argyris is the capitalist of the piece, exploiting the labour of his healthy, easy-going more proletarian brother and hated in the village for his profiteering; while his pious wizened 'mummy' of a wife, Chrysanthi, is permanently at loggerheads with her earthy sister-in-law Maria, whom she considers utterly beneath her and who in turn cannot abide Chrysanthi's airs and graces. And in the cat-and-mouse game with Thomas over an annuity in exchange for his property, Argyris swiftly gets the better of the old man, cunningly turning him against his own rightful heirs by playing on his hopes of amatory favours from Maria. Maria herself is a formidable village *femme fatale*, fun-loving, sexually manipulative, feisty in domestic quarrels and implacable when crossed — one of Theotokis's memorable half-emancipated women full of Nietzschean vitality. And once Thomas, like King Lear, has signed away his property and the promised perks are not forthcoming, he finds himself in thrall to her, exploited for his labour and taunted by the village children. The turning point comes with the climactic bedroom scene and Thomas's humiliation, after which the whole mood darkens and he resolves, Iago-like, to 'become a fiend' and eek his revenge upon the randy adolescent cousins. The finale in which Thomas returns from his lonely wanderings is poignant and there are Expressionist touches to his grotesque demise, which mirrors the earlier scene of his wife's death. Further light is cast on the whole psychodrama by the old notary's disclosures at the graveside.

A wealth of ethnographic information about Corfiot village life around 1900 is almost incidentally conveyed throughout the narrative. Argyris is very insistent on his status as 'helmsman' of the family, for instance, and the patriarchal nature of village society and subservience of women are humorously dramatized in the opening rumpus. The church's shortcomings receive a good socialist lambasting through the figure of the hypocritical and grasping priest, whose callous treatment of his father-in-law's destitute old paramour highlights the plight of the elderly, a major issue in the work. Chronic overcrowding, as common in such communities as in Corfu Town itself, motivates the entire action, with the brothers driven to escape from living 'hugger-mugger like the gypsies'. And its unhealthy and insanitary consequences are exemplified in Argyris's sickness and the condition of the corpse that so appalls the dresser. Peasant ignorance and superstition are alluded to repeatedly, for instance in Thomas's contention that sexual frustration leads to consumption, or Chrysanthi's fear of omens, ghosts and vampires. Insights into kinship obligations, dowries, wills and funerals abound; the problem of incest and inbreeding in such remote communities is raised; and the interconnected family histories of the protagonists provide a diachronic dimension largely absent from the *Corfiot tales*, while the daily and seasonal activities of fetching water, spinning, harvesting and minding sheep, the characteristic movements and habits of the animals, and the sounds and smells of village life amid the olive groves and vineyards are all briefly yet vividly evoked.

Like Conrad's *Heart of darkness* (1902), another short work that plumbs the depth of human depravity, Theotokis's novel is rich in symbolic details, which recur like Wagnerian leitmotifs orchestrated around the title's polarities of life and death.[6] Telling quirks of character or dress are repeated formulaically and proleptic images and scenes of gasping, choking and strangling recur throughout. Some particulars like Thomas's drooping phallic cigarette, or the guttering lamp during his vigil by his dying wife are in the mode of late Victorian fiction, others like his sowing tares or the wilting of Maria's vine are biblical in origin. Thomas is constantly associated with animals, particularly the goat and boar, symbols of lust since pagan times, and his spiritual trajectory is from Adam tempted, through Samson shorn, to satanic Tempter doomed to despair. His sensitivity to his nickname, a catalyst in many dramatic scenes, is symptomatic of how *philotimo*, or self-esteem, may become demonic pride in honour cultures, where men are quick to take offence and vengeance can spiral into a death cult — matters explored extensively in the *Corfiot tales*.[7]

But despite the almost Juvenalian harshness of the satire, *The life and*

---

[6] Theotokis first became acquainted with Wagner's music on his honeymoon in 1893, when according to his wife he was deeply impressed by a performance of *Lohengrin* in Munich.

[7] The common ground and regional and class differences between various patriarchal honour codes are explored in Gilmore, *Honor and shame and the unity of the Mediterranean*.

*death of Hangman Thomas* is a deeply compassionate work which enriches our understanding of the inner lives and circumscribed existence of these peasants without becoming overly tendentious or schematic. Theotokis's attitude towards even his most obnoxious characters tends to be complex and ambivalent. Thomas, for instance, for all his blind rages, lust and violence, is neither unmitigated villain nor buffoon, and (in compliance with Aristotle's prescription for the tragic hero) inspires pity and fear in equal measure.[8] He is increasingly identified with and devoted to his donkey — associated with the Devil in some parts of Greece, but also connected with the life of Christ; and the scene in which he runs the gauntlet of the hostile village mounted on its back is perhaps a reminder that he is more sinned against than sinning and — as he himself believes — being unjustly crucified by the community. The closest the narrative comes to a normative figure is the sunny sleepy Yannis, with his manly Greek moustache and gentle way with children, at once a symbol of the sleeping proletariat and a kindred spirit to the innocent Dostoevskian hero of *The convict*. But his improvidence, his deference to his scheming brother and his nickname 'Dunce-cap' indicate that there are no moral absolutes in this bleak fictive world, where suffering brings little compassion or enlightenment to anyone. What is indisputable is that Theotokis's overriding purpose in *The life and death of Hangman Thomas* is to present a vision of 'unaccommodated man' such as Shakespeare — whom he translated, admired and sought to emulate — might have endorsed.

## A NOTE ON THE TRANSLATION

Considering that Theotokis himself was an internationalist, some of whose translations — particularly his rendering of Flaubert's *Madame Bovary* — are still highly regarded, it is perhaps ironic that comparatively little of his own outstanding fiction has so far been translated, despite the early appearance of two of his novels in French as *Le condamné*

---

[8] Aristotle, *Poetics* 1449b, 1452a (tr. Stephen Halliwell, Loeb Classical Library, Harvard University Press, 1995, 47, 69f). The neoclassical unities of time, place and action derived from Aristotle are also adhered to fairly closely in this novel.

(1929) and *L'honneur et l'argent* (1933), both translated by Léon Krajewski. This is the first English translation of *The life and death of Hangman Thomas*, stylistically a less experimental work than the longer polyphonic urban novel, *Slaves in their chains* (also now available in English: see the Bibliography), but equally challenging to translate because of its extensive use of vigorous idiomatic speech and colourful religious, family and sexual imprecations.

True to his socialist objective of reaching as wide a readership as possible, Theotokis wrote in fairly standard demotic Greek, so that there are relatively few regional or dialectal terms to contend with. Some words for ethnic apparel like *tsarouchia* (pointed rustic shoes) have been left untranslated when clear from the context, others which occur more frequently like *bolia* (an elaborate woman's headdress which includes a *merza*, or long ribbon plaited into the hair) have been inadequately rendered by 'headscarf', so as not to impede the flow. Idioms almost always involve compromise: 'horses for courses', meaning that circumstances differ, sounds more English than 'all one's fingers are not the same length' (*olla ta daktyla den ine isia*), but it is not perfect in the village context, despite Argyris's patrician airs. The closest equivalent to *spolati sas* is the Irish and Australian 'good on you', which will sound more natural to some readers than to others. Kinship terms are more elaborate and more commonly used as direct forms of address in Greek than in English, and some references to, say, a person's sister-in-law or wife's bridesmaid have been trimmed. Chants in rhyming couplets (*mantinades*), exorcisms and curses with specific honour-code or religious connotations all tend to lose vigour in translation. When Maria for instance reproaches her husband for his phlegmatic reaction to their daughter's shame with 'Damn it Statiris, have you no pride!' this works dramatically, but it loses the acrimony of the Greek 'Ah you, Statiris, accustomed to dishonour' (*mathimene stin atimia*).

Theotokis is a nuanced writer who exploits the Greek language's potential for highly condensed expression to the full, and puns and double entendre can pose problems. When Thomas for instance refuses to sell off his capital he says: 'Woe to him who yields and touches it, it quickly vanishes like pollen . . . Puff!' But the first clause in Greek, *Alimono tou ekeinou pou glykathi ke vali cheri* could also be translated: 'Woe to him who softens (*or* sweetens) and begins to fondle (*or* grope)' — an ironic reference to his fateful relations with Maria. Or again, when Thomas first suspects his nickname is being alluded to, the consonance in Greek is between *karavelas* (hangman) and *karveli* (loaf), so that to get the same effect in English involves transposing the wordplay to the 'hanging larder' in which Maria keeps her bread.

One recurrent syntactic feature of *The life and death of Hangman Thomas* is the use of sentences with strings of short main clauses, and in some cases subordination has been necessary for the prose to sound natural in English. The clusters of adjectives used formulaically to identify characters each time they reappear have also occasionally been redistributed or trimmed for the same reason. But in general the original syntax and length of sentences has been respected.

Cadence is an additional concern for the translator. Theotokis, like Solomos, was brought up speaking both Greek and (that most musical of languages) Italian; and his early Aestheticist fiction, particularly the rhapsodic *Passion*, though a little stilted to the modern ear, reflects his interest in the musical potentialities of prose. *The life and death of Hangman Thomas* is rich in this regard and the racy idiomatic dialogue, brooding internal monologues, squalid Naturalist descriptions and lyrical evocations of the Corfiot landscape all have their own peculiar euphonic rhythm. The challenge is to find something that sounds equally natural in English, while resigning oneself to the fact that translation is at best a simulacrum.

The edition on which this translation is based is *I zoi ke o thanatos tou Karavela*, edited by Spyros Kokkinis (1990). The main sources consulted for the biographical and critical sections of this Introduction are *The early years of Konstantions Theotokis* by the author's brother, Spyridon M. Theotokis (1983), and the standard scholarly works by Emilios Chourmouzios and Yannis Dallas (all in Greek, full details in the Bibliography).

I should like to thank George Georghallides, Anthony Hirst and my wife Poh Pheng for their invaluable criticism and suggestions.

J. M. Q. Davies
Sydney, 2016

# THE LIFE AND DEATH

# OF

# HANGMAN THOMAS

*An asterisk in the text indicates that a note will be found at the back of the book relating to the preceding words. Each note begins with the page number in question, followed by the extract from the text.*

# I

Yannis and Argyris were brothers, the Statiris brothers. Still inseparable, they lived in the same house, each with his own family, high up in the village in a neighbourhood which sprawled halfway up the hill. Their house was a spruce white building, with two storeys facing downhill at the front and a single storey at the back; the long front wall had four windows, all freshly painted green, which looked out above a sturdy wooden trellis with a flourishing green vine. Beneath the trellis, a large wide door gave access to the store rooms and the stable, to which the sheep, a goat and two pigs would return at night, while the entrance to the residential part of the house was around the back and opened directly into a large living-room with two windows, off which were two smaller rooms to left and right, one occupied by Yannis the other by Argyris.

The brothers had both been married for years. Argyris, the elder, was a tall, pale corpulent man of forty, with a round clean-shaven face, small restless dark eyes, a trim moustache above thick lips, large plump hands and a huge paunch which hitched his black trousers well above his ankles and prevented him from buttoning his waistcoat and thick jacket. Summer and winter, Argyris always wore heavy woollen clothes, as he was convinced that all ailments started with a chill and he would often maintain that people caught cold more easily in summer, particularly those like himself who were in poor health, having been plagued for years with asthma, especially when upset or trying to work or struggling up the hill. This indeed was why he always carried a stout walking-stick, never took off his large patrician boater, and always talked softly in his ugly effeminate voice lest he overtax himself; and since he liked to appear grave and reasonable, he would also speak unhurriedly, tilting his head back, closing his little eyes and fluttering his eyelids.

Yannis resembled him a lot of course, but he was also very different and a good deal younger. He too was stout, but shorter, more robust and ruddy of complexion; his voice was rough, he dressed more coarsely and in general his demeanour was more plebeian and uneducated. His small dark eyes were cheerful, half-closed and always moist, his rosy lips wore a perpetual smile which exposed his blackened yellow teeth, and his drooping moustache curled about his chin; often he would hold his straw hat in his hand, displaying his well-combed curly hair, and in hot weather he would sling his jacket over one shoulder and leave his waistcoat and crumpled white shirt unbuttoned, exposing his sunburned hairy chest. In the village Yannis was known as a hard worker and he danced better than any of the other men, his straw hat tilted rakishly over one ear and looking far too small for his large head. Everybody called him 'Dunce-cap' and ever since childhood he had grown so accustomed to the nickname that he no longer took offence.*

It was the beginning of summer and noon was approaching. Argyris had just returned home and, after putting his stick in a corner and removing his boater from his perspiring brow, he collapsed heavily into a chair by the table in the middle of the room, his fat legs spread out in front of him, his head tilted back, his pale lips gasping for air. He was out of breath after walking up the hill and fanned himself with his handkerchief, turning his face from side to side. It was a while before he recovered, but finally he took a deep breath, and fluttering his eyelids called out to his sister-in-law in his ugly high-pitched voice, 'Maria! Maria!'

'Coming!' replied an attractive female voice from the kitchen, which was in a separate outhouse opposite the main entrance and built against the hillside.

A moment later a tall dark-haired scrumptious woman, no longer in the first flush of youth, came into the living-room. Her eyes were black and lively, her rosy cheeks as yet unlined and her lips thin but very red. Her head was loosely draped in a white headscarf and her homespun woollen skirt was hitched above her knees, the hem tucked into her belt, leaving the bottom of her long gray smock exposed.

'What is it, wha'd'ya want?' she asked, speaking so rapidly a stranger might have had difficulty understanding her.

'Water for a start!' he replied, still panting and licking his dry lips.

'Wa-a-a-ter, eh!' she replied with a mocking smile. 'All the water you keep drinking like an ox, that's what makes you ill, you know. Take it from me, it rots the gut — that's only natural! Look at wood: what happens to it in the damp? It'll last a year or two ... Ten if you're lucky, but in the end it too will rot, because that's the way wood is ...

Now if you'd brought back some cognac, I'd have joined you; but water, I never touch it! — not even at the well! ... What landlord ever drinks water, besides your good self? ... It's only fit for beggars. As for me, I sell a few eggs now and then and so never go short of cognac or raki — an egg per swig. It helps revive me! So naturally in the afternoon ... I occasionally have a nip!'

Meanwhile she had filled a large glass from the water-pitcher on the windowsill and handed it to him.

'Don't drink it right away,' she added, 'you're overheated. It might make you worse! And ailments, God preserve us, are infectious!'

But Argyris paid no attention to her, downed the water in one draft, heaved a sigh and closed his little eyes contentedly. Then wiping his moustache with his hand he asked, 'How's lunch, ready yet?'

'Any minute now — your wife will call us,' she replied.

After that they both fell silent. Argyris's attack of asthma gradually subsided and he was able to pause and reflect. Tilting back his large round head and blinking his little eyes, he asked her, 'By the way, did you get a chance to discuss that little matter with them?'

'Yes,' she replied casually, pursing her red lips, 'but it looks as if nothing can be settled! I talked to my sister, the priest's wife, but got nowhere! She says she's discussed it with her husband, but to no avail. As regards our father, she says, who cares if he agrees or not, because, she says, what can the poor old codger do about it anyway. Willy-nilly, he'll have to toe the line. But the priest, she says, definitely needs the house — the whole of it — and if, she says, we insist on having a share of it, then nothing can be settled. Nothing. The priest intends to arrange for his son to marry soon, as he wants him to become a priest as well,* and to avoid domestic friction he plans to add another storey to the house. They need the space. So he's hardly going to let us have half! ... He's calculating that if we don't divide things now, in time he'll be able to persuade my father to make a will and so ensure my sister keeps the house. That's what they're aiming for. But if we agree to let them have the house now, then my sister is willing to compensate us with land, and the division can go ahead ... Would it were tomorrow. I didn't of course commit myself, as it seems a serious matter, don't you think? Why shouldn't I get something in bricks and mortar from my father too, even if we already have a house, half this one, that is ... So I wanted to consult you — or rather my husband —

after all, what's it got to do with you?'

Argyris went a little paler and gave her a wry look. Just then Yannis came in, his jacket slung over one shoulder, his open shirt exposing his sunburned chest. He looked the picture of rosy-cheeked good health. Maria greeted him with a ready smile, looking him up and down admiringly and glancing at his brother with contempt.

'Deep in conversation, eh!' said Dunce-cap.

And he laughed: 'Ha! ha! ha!' with eyes half closed.

Argyris looked him in the eye reproachfully.

'Tipsy again, eh?' he remarked. 'Found someone to tipple with again today? And before lunch too? One more down the hatch . . . eh?'

Maria flushed and tossed her head resentfully. Argyris's remarks annoyed her. She did not like him upbraiding her husband, who after all was not a little boy! If he drank, so what; he watched what he spent and had a right to enjoy himself as he saw fit! He didn't need permission!

Addressing her husband, she said seriously. 'He's been asking about the division with my sister, you see.'

'Their father,' said Argyris, blinking nervously and weighing every word, 'doesn't need to be consulted; that's what the priest says and of course he's absolutely right. Because once the division is decided, each sister will take over her share at once, and then what's the old notary going to do? Fly off the handle? Well, that will soon blow over. Supposing he still wants access to his fields and olive groves and houses! . . . fine, let him have it, what's to prevent him! But suppose he wants to sell his property, ah, well that's another matter! . . . Who would buy it! What outsider would be in a hurry to bid for property encumbered in that way? He'd have to be mad! . . . Same with renting: he'd never find a tenant! So what it all boils down to is the disagreement over the house. Your brother-in-law, the priest, wants the whole house for himself and of course will give you land in compensation; now it's up to you to agree to the division, he says, and then things can be settled right away! To my mind, that is in your interest!'

'Oh, do what you like!' replied Yannis laughing, too bored to give it further thought. 'Let the priest give us what he wants, d'you really think I care? Here's how much!' — and he flicked his tooth with his fingernail.*

'We've food aplenty in this family, thank God, so why should I worry my head about such things, just to catch consumption?* Not on your life! Yannis looks after his health because he's very fond of Yannis — very fond indeed!'

And he laughed heartily.

Argyris made no reply and continued to look thoughtful, then after a few moments he looked up, his little eyes blinking, and asked quietly, 'And how is Thomas's wife?'

'Ah, dear God,' replied Maria sadly, 'she's more dead than alive, poor thing! Who knows, by this evening, or perhaps tomorrow, it's touch and go . . .'

And she wobbled her right hand with fingers cupped.

'A shame!' said Yannis. 'Such a good neighbour . . .'

'Very good!' Argyris nodded gravely, 'good for us too, perhaps! . . . If we contrived things the way I have suggested and acquired Thomas's house for ourselves, we wouldn't need another house. In fact land would be more useful to us, as we could then grow a variety of crops! In which case why not divide things the way the priest proposes! If Thomas's wife does die, may God have mercy on her, I'd say the whole thing's by no means impossible! Thomas will be left alone and might well feel the need for our support . . .'

'He has nephews and nieces who are practically his own children,' said Yannis, sitting down on the doorstep and gazing out, 'so why even think about such things ? What do you want with such injustice?'

'You can have Thomas's house as your share of the property,' said Maria spitefully. 'We don't want it.'

'Fine, I'll have it,' said Argyris casually, 'why not, I'll have it! It makes no difference who has which half! Once we get it of course, we'll demolish it and rebuild it flush with this one so they match; we'll run the two houses into one, and then . . .'

'Ah, Argyris!' Maria interrupted, 'you're again thinking up schemes to work my poor Yannis into an early grave! More fool him for listening to you! If I were Yannis, I'd give the whole idea two fingers! But he's always been your mindless slave, poor fellow. You'll wear him out!'

Yannis laughed.

'One has to work to live!' replied Argyris gravely.

'We eat our fill,' sighed Maria, 'and he works his heart out all day long, poor man!'

'But whose head does all the planning, my good woman?' replied

Argyris proudly, going pale.

'Calm down now, don't get started,' said Yannis wearily. 'You pick the same time every day for your bickering and quarrels, poisoning our lives! Run along, Maria, for God's sake, leave us in peace, will you! . . .'

'Far better to divide things between you now as well,' declared Maria, 'then each knows who owns what . . . instead of carrying on like this! Now you're procrastinating over Thomas's inheritance! Oh, God! as things stand we'll acquire more property, we'll put in the work, then you'll go and divide it equally!'

'Well, I like that!' exclaimed Argyris, thoroughly ruffled. 'That's a bit rich! If I'd known and taken my share of whatever I acquired on your behalf from the beginning, everything would today belong to me, me and my children!'

'Everything was built with his backbreaking labour!' said Maria pointing to her husband. 'You're not fit for work — though of course that's not your fault!'

'All those years of misery, failed harvests and disasters,' Argyris continued, 'everyone went hungry, even the nobility, but in this family no one ever did without a thing! Admit it: not a thing! We continued accumulating wealth, a field here, a few olive trees there, now and then some stone towards the house we're planning, and all of it has raised our social standing! Thank God I kept a gimlet-eye on things day and night, in the interests of my children, and yours as well of course. And now you want us to divide things? Now? . . . Fine, that suits me too. How much did our father leave us? You know all about it, Yannis! Our older half-brothers kept the best pickings, including their mother's dowry, for themselves and got rid of us, lodging us and our mother in a miserable hovel — because as you remember, Yannis, this house was not in such good condition then, I had to do it up! And for years I was saddled with the two of you, she growing old and dotty and you still under age . . . What brother ever did as much? I could have gone my own way, but instead I fixed up the house for you, making your room even better than my own; I arranged your marriage and so far I've been bringing up your children, while you carry on regardless, sleeping and carousing! Tomorrow will take care of itself! . . . And now you both want to divide things; very well then, let's divide things! . . .'

'What rubbish you talk!' cried Maria angrily, 'it was all done with the sweat of his brow, with his hard work, simpleton that he is for doing everything you ask him! ... Are you fit for manual work? Answer me that! You're a sick man, aren't you? Not half! For years now you've been staggering about, puffing and wheezing, you miserable wretch! ... And you won't last much longer ... Damn me, if I'll listen to such nonsense!'

Argyris turned pale as death and gave an ugly laugh.

'Calm down, for God's sake, woman,' Yannis told her. 'Right on cue again!'

'Let her prattle on,' Argyris sighed. 'She doesn't bother me, God above is listening to every word! After all these years I know what she is like; I'm the one unjustly treated here, sick man though I am! ... But make sure you sort out the division with the priest, because I neither wish nor intend to wrong my children. And when we divide things, whether now or later on, make no mistake about it, our portions won't be equal ... Certainly not!'

'Won't be equal?' exclaimed Maria, her hackles again rising, 'they won't be equal, because Your Lordship will get less, of course, as you've not done any of the work! As you well know, your sickness ruled that out! Why don't you consider that your days are numbered, Argyris you poor wretch, instead of making your own brother moan about you, like so many others you have wronged?'

'To make sure you all ate well!' Argyris insisted with a bitter laugh.

'As if my husband needs you!' replied Maria proudly. 'He's the one who feeds us all! ... The other day you again pocketed the fifty drachmas he got for butchering that calf. Yet he brought meat home for all of us to eat. He'll be slaughtering again on Saturday, but this time you won't see a penny! Not a penny, I tell you! I too have daughters to find dowries for — how long am I supposed to wait? Females grow up quickly, already they're young fillies; when am I supposed to buy a bit of cloth for them? So don't expect another handout from that stupid Yannis! Wake up, Yannis, you simpleton; wake up, Dunce-cap!'

And seizing her husband by the shoulder, she shook him violently.

Here Argyris finally lost patience and going even paler laughed and said, 'Ha ha! This is one family and one person has to be in charge! We can't all be playing God! Just because I allow you to keep your own hens and sheep and goats, it doesn't mean you can control your own purse-strings too! A pretty pickle we would soon be in: everything would be topsy-turvy, just the way Maria likes it! ... '

'Well, divide things up then, so everybody knows what's his; that's what I've been saying for the last ten years!' exclaimed Maria, leaning forward slightly, arms akimbo .

'Right then, let's divide things up,' said Argyris, pale and trembling, 'though not equally of course. I've got all the accounts on file, each family's income and expenses. I get more land because my wife's dowry's larger and I only have two children to feed, whereas you have four!'

'He's remembered them!' cried Maria. 'And those wooden shacks belonging to his mummy of a wife! Jabber-jabber, jabber-jabber!'

Here she made a monkey face, opening and closing her mouth repeatedly.

'Mummy indeed!' exclaimed Argyris furiously. 'And what about her fields and olive groves and oil mills?'

'Yes, and we're the ones who work them!' Maria shouted at him, thrusting her head closer and slapping her left palm with three fingers of her right hand. 'You keep trotting out the same old arguments! I'm tired of hearing you. Argyris the unjust!'

'Are you going to bring her into line or not?' Argyris asked his brother, quite beside himself.

'What am I supposed to do?' replied Yannis with a shrug. 'Look at the way she's carrying on — like a supreme court judge!'

And he laughed.

'So you're in league, the two of you!' exclaimed Argyris, getting up.

But just then his wife, Chrysanthi, entered.

She was of middle height, about forty-five years old and very dry and wrinkled, with dead, hollow eyes and barely any teeth. Her wispy hair under her headscarf had started to turn white, her head drooped a little and wobbled when she spoke and her face was as always very pale.

'What's the matter, woman, what's all the fuss about?' she asked Maria angrily.

Maria gave her a fierce intimidating glance and shouted, evidently addressing her own husband, 'And rightly so! With Lord Argyris putting on his airs again. Rightly so! But then of course he married a rich woman . . . A woman of breeding!'

And she indicated Chrysanthi without so much as glancing at her.

'I'm far superior to you, you country bumpkin!' replied Chrysanthi. 'Goodness! Every day you pick this time to upset my poor dear husband and put him off his food! Why d'you do it, stupid, why?'

'His food!' Maria jeered. 'He grows fat on his injustices!' And she puffed her cheeks out. 'Don't you see he's become so bloated he can barely stagger up the hill? Look at him! . . . He's sick, poor fellow, you won't have him around much longer, I assure you! That's obvious. And that's why he's so evil! . . . He's envious of strong and healthy people! . . . He's all venomous inside, he's eaten up by malice. And he's given you consumption too! Yes, of course you are consumptive! That's why you're as pale as a cucumber! . . .'

'As for you and your good looks, Madam!' sneered Chrysanthi sourly, 'they're what led you from the straight and narrow! . . . Just hold your tongue, before I throw the good book at you! D'you think people have forgotten? Is that what you imagine? Don't fool yourself! Have you forgotten that you had no marriage prospects, and that if Argyris and I had not been there to hitch you to his brother, you'd have been on the shelf, you baggage, because no one would have had you! And now you make his life a misery! Well done, congratulations! Remember what you got up to with your cousin?* He was good looking too, of course! And they kept finding you together in the ditches . . . and . . . and . . . I could go on. And then Dunce-cap fell in love with you for your good looks and he's the one obliged to wear the horns! . . . Now come along and eat, everybody; holy Mary, what a to do, what a to-do! . . .'

'You old mummy!' Maria shouted at her furiously. 'Jabber-jabber, jabber-jabber. I tell you, malice has eaten both your hearts out!' And she thumped her chest. Then with mounting fury she went on: 'Here's where I make a note of everything you say!' and cocking her leg backwards, she gave her sole a good sharp slap. 'Argyris has infected you, you pathetic creature! Too late, you've got consumption! Look at my glowing cheeks, now my blood is up — even though Argyris never brings home any wine for us but sneaks it in for you. Think I don't know, eh? I don't turn pale when I get angry, but just look at your ugly mugs in the mirror over there, the two of you! Go on, take a look! And now look at the manly fellow who shares my bed! He's as ruddy as a pomegranate, long may he live! Look at him. Whereas your Argyris is bloodless down to his fingernails! He's tubercular, disgusting, rotten to the core, poor fellow!' And she spat on the ground. 'Very soon you'll both drop dead, you miserable creatures, and then we'll be lumbered with your orphaned children, but as for me, I'll dance on your graves like this!' And flinging her headscarf to the ground, she started dancing spryly and humming in imitation of a violin.

'Stop this farce, for God's sake!' said Argyris sweating with rage, his voice trembling and distinctly higher. 'If you, Dunce-cap, can't knock some sense into her, I will! ... We agreed that whenever the wives started quarrelling you'd beat mine and I'd beat yours!'* And he glared at Maria, puffing and panting.

'That mummy of yours would still be better off,' cried Maria, 'because my Yannis is a good, kind hearted and compassionate man! But you? ... well, God help me!'

'As for me, I am absolutely famished,' declared Yannis laughing. And he hastily got up and left the room, without so much as glancing back.

'Statiris, you cuckold!' Maria shouted after him, stamping her foot. 'Just you wait! We'll have this out in bed! You'll get what's coming to you ...'

'Hit her!' Chrysanthi urged her husband gleefully. 'Be a saint and give her a good hiding!'

'You old mummy!' screamed Maria, 'Jabber-jabber, jabber-jabber!'

'You first,' Argyris told his wife. 'What d'you mean by interfering? D'you want the whole neighbourhood to hear us, eh?' And with this he gave her a sound backhanded slap.

Chrysanthi immediately burst into clamorous tears and sank to the floor beside the chest, her face buried in her hands.

'And now for you, Maria!' said Argyris panting, and seizing her by her headscarf he started shaking her with all his might.

She uttered a loud piercing scream, then muttered between clenched teeth, 'Confound your whole damn clan, Argyris!'

Finally she cried out, 'Help, someone! Argyris is trying to kill me. It's Argyris, neighbours, yes, Argyris!'

But her screams did not deter him and he went on shaking her, whereupon she cried, 'I won't submit to you, Argyris, damn it ... Yes, I was right, you're rotten to the core; you don't even have the strength to beat me, you pathetic creature! What a man! Look how pale you've gone! You've had it, you'll drop dead any minute ... Normal people go red when they get angry, but you turn white as chalk ... Ah, you ... Don't hit so hard, you wimp! You'll blister your own hands! Don't, I tell you, or you'll have that stroke the doctor warned you of. Then byebye Argyris! That scared you, eh? Ouch! Ouch! Ouch!'

By this stage Argyris was completely out of breath. His rage and his exertions had made him sweat profusely and his face was as pale as a corpse. Suddenly he let go of her and collapsed into his chair, his round head tilted back, his pale lips gasping as he looked around for help.

'Murderess, you've killed him!' wailed Chrysanthi, who was by his side at once. 'Look what you've done to him! Ah, may God punish you for this!'

She embraced Argyris, stroked his head and fanned his face with her headscarf, anxiously observing his restless yellowish eyes.

'You've killed him!'

'Devil take him then!' shouted Maria spitefully and burst out laughing.

Then pretending to be overjoyed, she skipped out of the door and into the kitchen to have her lunch.

'After everything I've done for them,' Argyris whispered faintly, 'I still have to put up with this.'

And his eyes rolled back, leaving only the whites showing. Then after several anxious moments, he said to his wife quietly, 'I might go and lie down! Ugh! Ugh!'

With an effort he managed to heave his heavy body out of the chair and, leaning on her arm, slowly shuffled to their room and stretched out on the bed, loosening his clothes so as to breathe more easily. Chrysanthi took off his shoes for him and then stood silently beside the bed.

'You may go,' he told her after a while. 'I feel better now. Otherwise she'll finish off the food and we'll go hungry. Make sure you put some aside for Thomas. Call him and serve it him yourself. And tell him to come and see me, I want to have a chat with him.'

'Such a good soul,' sighed Chrysanthi admiringly, 'not a thought for himself, poor man, flat on his back thanks to her wickedness, yet providing charity for Thomas... Such a good soul! You'll ascend to heaven alive one of these fine days.' And she began to weep, her head wobbling a little. 'Ah, the way that family treats you!...' she went on, 'yet you refuse to have done with them and strike out on your own to relax a little! Why don't you take things easier, it's for their sake, isn't it?'

'They do the work,' Argyris muttered sourly, 'if we split up, we'd have to take on outside labour, so we'd be feeding and paying wages to outsiders.* Go on, off with you! . . .'

Chrysanthi stood beside the bed a moment longer, looking at her husband thoughtfully; then shaking her head sadly she slowly left the room.

# II

In the kitchen, Yannis was seated at the bare table on a narrow wooden bench, with his back to the door and facing the wall; he was still eating hungrily, bending over his deep plate, getting gravy onto his moustache, smacking his lips and snorting through his nostrils as he tended to do when sleeping. Maria was sitting next to him but with her back to him, leaning against the table and steadying her plate on her knees with one hand while holding her wooden spoon in the other. She was not on speaking terms with him.

Outside the door, her daughter was sitting on the ground sewing, her bare feet stretched out in front of her. She was a tall, pretty, fair-haired girl of fourteen with her mother's rosy complexion and good figure. Just then her head was bent over the white fabric she was holding taut between her knees, and she appeared to be concentrating on her needlework. She was without a headscarf, her sleeves were rolled up and the threads for her embroidery were draped around her neck.

Leaning against the wall opposite her, likewise sitting on the ground, was Andreas, a tall lanky youth of sixteen with long legs, rounded shoulders, a clear skin and rosy cheeks, but with an unusually wide mouth and large teeth. Andreas was also fair-haired and had big bright eyes flecked with russet gold. The two cousins had been devoted ever since childhood and always played alone together, and just then they were teasing one another, giggling surreptitiously and looking into one another's eyes.* Every now and then, Andreas would pinch her or embrace her and try to snatch the bead she wore on a black thread around her neck; Maria, still in a foul temper, watched them out of the corner of her eye, but said nothing, because even at that age she did not want to put deceitful ideas into her daughter's head. Such had been Argyris's advice, and Yannis had laughingly agreed.

Suddenly Maria called out 'Olga!' to her other, much younger daughter, who was also outside the door playing with her two little brothers.

As soon as the girl, a pretty eleven-year-old already dressed in adult clothes, came in, her mother said to her, 'Here's some change, go and fetch me a little wine so I can relax... But wash the bottle first... And make sure you don't drink a single drop yourself, or I'll tan your hide!'

'Yes, Mum!' said the girl shyly and turned to go.

'Our menfolk,' continued Maria provokingly, 'go drinking down at the wine-store and we get nothing... They expect us to make do with water. And yet Argyris secretly brings wine home for that old mummy of his!...'

Yannis laughed, wiping his moustache, and said, 'Give her enough for me as well.'

Maria turned away from him abruptly, hiding her face behind her headscarf, and said, 'Tell him, Olga, to petition Lord Argyris, his dear brother, for anything he wants... Yes, the brother who leaves him without a penny in his pocket... What confounded cheek! Ha, ha! Pretending we've already forgotten everything that happened earlier, are we!... Well, I'll have you know, Olga, I don't forgive that easily. Let Lord Argyris fetch it for him, since he's given him authority to beat his wife... Let him do his wifely chores as well.'

The two young people, Amalia and Andreas, burst out laughing, amused by her heated indignation, while Yannis, pretending not to hear, leaned over, craning his neck as he tried to look into her face. Glimpsing him out of the corner of her eye, she flushed and again turned away abruptly.

For a few moments no one spoke. Yannis finished off his food, wiped his mouth again and slowly turned around until his elbow touched his wife. She flushed red and looked away again, then suddenly got to her feet, shoved her plate into the middle of the table and with her hands on her hips said, 'Get up, Amalia, girl, and take your sheep off down to graze. You're all driving me insane today... And don't forget your sewing,* so at least you be getting on with that as well! Letting the sheep starve to death like this... it's a sin for God's sake!...'

'We'll both go,' said her cousin.

The two of them were on their feet at once.

'That won't be necessary!... That won't be necessary!...' Maria told the lad, shaking her head stubbornly, 'I don't like all this gallivanting... and your traipsing after her all day!... I'm fed up with it!... You're not children any longer! Besides, we know whose son you are . . .'

'Come now,' laughed Yannis, again trying to break the ice, 'they are practically brother and sister . . . Why put ideas into their heads!'

'The fact is, Andreas,' Maria continued, pointedly ignoring her husband, 'you come from lousy stock and I have to take precautions.'

Andreas laughed, offended, then leaning over he whispered into his cousin's ear, 'I'll join you down there! . . . Off you go! . . .'

And the two cousins gazed into one another's eyes and smiled. Maria meanwhile went on talking: 'You know, Andreas, I'm a clever woman . . . I wouldn't exchange my brains with the best of men! If only others were a little more like me! . . .'

A moment later, glancing out of the door, she cried, 'Amalia, damn you, where are your little brothers off to?'

'School.'

'And what about your sister, Andreas? Ah, she's being groomed for higher things, of course, she's destined for a wealthy family, don't you know! Ha, ha! But sometimes the donkey and his master disagree.* You all seem to have forgotten that! . . .'

'She left as soon as you all started quarrelling,' replied Andreas with a grin. 'She didn't even have lunch and just took some bread. She doesn't find these rows much fun . . .'

He laughed and watched Amalia as she bent to gather up her sewing and put it in her basket.

'Don't dawdle,' said her mother. 'Hurry up!'

The girl fastened her distaff so that she could spin while walking, swung her basket onto her head and stepped out of the door; and from the kitchen they could hear her voice for a little while coaxing the sheep to follow her.

Just then Olga returned from the store with the wine and as she entered yelled out, 'Hangman Thomas is coming!'

'May cankers rot your mouth,' her mother shouted angrily, accustomed to cursing her female progeny robustly. 'Haven't I told you, perish your soul, never to call him that? If he hears you, all hell will break loose! You know he can't abide that nickname, it makes him absolutely rabid! Why can't you hold your tongue? Besides, he's an elderly man and you ought to respect him like your father — more than your father!'

And turning to Yannis, she exclaimed dismissively, 'Bah! Bah!'

'Besides,' she added, 'he might do us a good turn, as I've explained to you before, he could become our benefactor!'

'Your mother's right,' said Yannis seriously, but giving her a conspiratorial wink.

Just then Thomas appeared, slowly approaching his front door with measured steps.

He was a man of about sixty, but still vigorous and in good health. Short and sturdy, though a little stooped, he had white hair, a ruddy complexion, large soft slightly bloodshot eyes and wild bushy eyebrows which were also turning white, as was his long thinning moustache above his sensuous rosy lips. He was wearing thick blue cotton breeches down to his knees, dirty white stockings, *tsarouchia* with no pompoms on his feet,* a black double-breasted waistcoat fastened with three silver buttons, a broad sky-blue sash around his waist and a large untrimmed straw hat pulled low over his brow, concealing his face completely as he trudged along with head downcast.

'Welcome, Thomas!' said Yannis with a smile.

'Welcome, dear Thomas!' said Maria sweetly.

'Good day to you both,' he replied, gazing at Maria with a sigh.

As the old man entered, Andreas chuckled to himself, relishing the thought of what would happen if anyone should call him by his nickname now; then glancing at Maria to make sure he was no longer being watched, he said to himself, 'I'm off!' and slipped out through the door unnoticed.

'And Angela? How is she?' asked Maria with concern.

'More dead than alive, I'm afraid!' said Thomas. 'By this evening, perhaps by tomorrow...' And as he said this he wobbled his cupped right hand. 'But to tell the truth, my dear Maria,' he went on, 'the sooner the better, the state she's in. She's aged so much, so very much... She's no use for anything any longer! Anything at all!' And he smiled insinuatingly. 'In fact, these last few days,' he added, 'she's become incontinent and fouls her bed.' And here he spat. 'The bedding's rotting... you have no idea!'

Maria too spat on the ground, wiping her lips with the corner of her headscarf.

Yannis laughed abruptly and remarked, 'Sad, how people can end up!'

'She's grown old, old and senile,' Thomas went on, looking Maria in the eye.

'And so, Thomas,' she replied, 'you'll be left all alone — a monk! . . . Poor Thomas!'

'Who knows what fate may have in store for me,' said Thomas, turning his palms outwards as he shrugged. 'Who knows! . . .'

'At your age . . .' observed Yannis laughing.

'You wouldn't be on the lookout for another woman, would you?' asked Maria smiling archly. 'I believe you are. A game cock, old Thomas, despite his venerable age . . .'

'Well, if I were to find someone suitable,' chuckled the old man, 'someone in her prime of course, like your good self, let's say, who knows what I might do!'

'Ah, so you fancy me, do you?' said Maria, spitefully looking her husband in the eye as she touched her rosy cheeks. Then she laughed. 'Won't you have a drop, then, Thomas?'

Yannis too laughed heartily.

'I've not eaten yet,' said Thomas.

Just then Chrysanthi came into the kitchen, stooping, her whole body shaking, her face pale. Maria glanced at her with hatred and turned away contemptuously. Disconcerted, the other woman went even paler, but greeted Thomas and having enquired after his sick wife said, 'My husband heard you were here and told me to offer you a meal, as you won't be getting cooked food at home with your wife ill. We've saved some for you.'

'Good on you,' replied Thomas, 'but may I eat it here as well? If I take it over, I'll have to share it with my sister, who has come to nurse the invalid. And then . . . She can make do with bread . . . though today we're out of that as well. Perhaps I might borrow some! . . .'

'There's some in the hanging larder,' said Maria and immediately bit her tongue.

'Hanging! Hanging!' muttered Thomas, flushing suddenly and looking round.

'Hanging!' he repeated, feeling he was about to lose control and fly into a rage, as he was reminded of his nickname.

The two sisters-in-law looked askance at one another, forgetting their mutual enmity at once. Yannis could scarcely contain his laughter, but aware that the old man would never forgive them if he knew they too were making fun of him, he managed to contain himself. With a straight face, Maria proceeded to take a large flat yellowish cob out of the hanging larder, while Chrysanthi silently ladled his dinner onto a plate, placed it on the table next to where Yannis was still sitting and herself withdrew to the hearth with a slice of bread. There she scraped what little cooked food remained onto a plate and started eating very slowly, as her lack of teeth made chewing difficult. Thomas also now began to eat in silence.

After a while Maria poured him half a glass of wine, saying 'Drink.'

'Good health,' he replied, taking the glass from her and raising it.

'And a pure soul!' added Chrysanthi in her tremulous voice.

The old man looked at her wryly as he put his glass to his lips. 'Ah no,' he thought, 'I don't want to die.'

'To your marriage, Thomas!' smiled Maria, winking at him.

He gave her a fond appreciative look and sipped his wine. Yannis laughed again.

'And the rest for me! . . .' Maria continued, raising the bottle to her lips. 'No more for others. Let those with money go and buy some more! . . . It's available down at the store . . . Good health to you, Thomas!'

She tilted her head right back, steadying her headscarf with her left hand, and slowly poured the wine straight from the bottle into her mouth.

Then they all fell silent and watched Thomas tucking in with gusto.

After a while, Chrysanthi said to him in a low voice, 'My husband asked if you'd drop in and see him, he's expecting you. They've upset him again today, God punish them, and the poor man couldn't eat. He collapsed into bed and has been resting ever since, but he's made a special effort to get up because he wants to speak to you. He's very fond of you, Thomas, my dear husband, he's a good soul, poor fellow, and thinks of you a lot, you're always on his lips. And your poor wife as well.'

Thomas paused between spoonfuls and smiled. 'I'll go and see him,' he told her with his mouth full.

Maria looked daggers at Chrysanthi and muttered to herself, 'The viper! The evil schemer!'

Then everyone again fell silent. Thomas polished off his meal without another word. Maria busied herself about the kitchen, collecting the wooden spoons, thick plates, cooking pots and iron cutlery ready to be washed; then she swept the yard and filled a large jug from the water-pitcher. Chrysanthi kept nodding off as she slowly chewed her food, while Yannis got ready to go down to the store.

At last Thomas wiped his mouth, crossed himself and got to his feet.

'I'll just take the bread round to my sister first,' he said, 'and then I'll go and see Argyris.'

'As you wish,' replied Chrysanthi meekly. 'We'll be expecting you.'

'See you later,' said Maria coyly.

He gave her a radiant smile and squeezed her hand.

'By this evening,' he remarked, 'or tomorrow at the latest, she'll have passed away . . .'

And again he smiled.

A little later Thomas found himself engaged in serious conversation with Argyris in the main room of the house. Argyris was still quite pale and having difficulty breathing as he lay back in his chair, his hands supporting his fat head. Thomas was standing in front of him and holding forth.

'Don't take it all so much to heart,' he was saying, 'I'm advising you as if you were my son, don't vent your spleen so often, you'll only harm yourself, nursing your grievances all day. What will become of you? Look at me, I cool down at once, I put it all behind me and that way I'm still as fit as a young lad. Wouldn't you agree?'

'Ah, that sister-in-law of mine,' Argyris sighed, 'she's so cantankerous . . . And who needs that . . . Always cursing, shouting and carrying on! . . .'

'Like a mare released from the stable . . .' said Thomas, his eyes sparkling. And a moment later he added thoughtfully, 'Women need the rod. Only the rod will tame them. They say there was a rod in Paradise, yes, slap in the middle.* There's a hymn that mentions it as well — I don't know which of course, I'm not a theologian, but anyway! . . . And men should never get splenetic and upset, nursing their grievances and poisoning themselves. No, sir! Anger is quite different:* there a man goes red in the face, starts yelling, comes to blows and then cools down. Over and done with! Spleen is another matter: it settles in a man's vitals, collects in his heart and turns it bilious and rots it! That's what happens to somebody splenetic. I, my friend, never get splenetic, I'm not an inward-looking man, you see,

I'm not malicious, I don't bottle my emotions up. No, sir. With my old woman, whenever I got angry I would beat her, my word yes, I would give her a real hiding. By St Spyridon,* I wouldn't spare the rod when she deserved it... Would you? Especially of late, since she's grown old and, if I may say so, completely useless... May she depart sooner rather than later, since it can't be helped; rather her than me. Isn't that right? Pity about the suckling babes she might have left behind, ha, ha, ha!' And he chuckled.

'It won't be long,' replied Argyris, closing his eyes as if terrified by the very idea of death, 'and that's only natural, now she has grown old. But I wanted to ask you: have you made provision for your good self? The one who dies has no further needs, but the one surviving has to eat, drink and go on living!'

'I've done everything you advised me to a while ago,' replied Thomas. 'She was still alright then. I say alright! My God! She could just about drag herself around. It's only in the last six months that she's been bedridden. We went over to the notary's together, shuffling along, taking a good two hours to get there. And it's scarcely a stone's throw, as you know. People stared and laughed at us. I was fuming but restrained myself, otherwise they'd have started their catcalling and nicknames... Anyway, finally we got there. And the notary, your brother's father-in-law, drew up a will in highfaluting language, stating that whoever predeceased the other would leave everything to the survivor. If I died first, that is, she would be my heir. But how could I predecease her, for God's sake? Even then she was struggling to breathe, while I was and remain healthy and robust... and I'm younger too... Then again, I told myself, if I were destined to go first, well that would be that, what could I do? But there we are, things have turned out as I predicted. Now I'm inheriting from her. Oh, small potatoes, I assure you. Country chattels aren't much of a dowry!... Still... why must I now have to have her relations round my neck? Endless disputes at home over inventories, accounts and what not... having to return the smocks she wore out twenty years ago... itemizing everything... No end of trouble! But that's the law, God help us! Whoever drafted it should have been strangled. Yes, strangled, along with all the other legislators. But as things are, her heirs can suck their thumbs for consolation. Her sister has a whole brood of children, lucky woman, unlike my Angela she wasn't barren... Such has been my fate . . . She has two sons, tall strapping fellows, and I don't know how many daughters — the last one a surprise! . . .'

'Four,' said Argyris closing his eyes: he was familiar with all the local families and what property they owned. 'But bear something else in mind now, Thomas: you know I love you like a father . . . You said as much yourself . . .'

'God bless you,' he replied with a sly smile that showed he did not believe a word of it. 'I know you love me, yes, good on you . . .' And he paused a moment, waiting to hear what Argyris would say next.

'Well, what did you want to talk to me about?' he asked eventually.

'You say you have escaped her heirs, but now you must be wary of your own. Your nephews and nieces are good worthy people, as is your sister and her husband, an honourable family, who would deny it? Sober decent people, all of them! But they too will want you to go and live with them, so they can look after you in your old age; that's what they'll say of course . . . and it's only natural that you should go to them . . . What will you do all on your own? Yes, by all means you should go, of course you should . . . Only . . . After all, who else d'you have besides your nephews to support you?'

'Support me?' interrupted Thomas testily. 'Let them support their own parents if they wish!'

'Well, who else do you have, since you are childless? But then . . . You'll be entering murky waters, my poor Thomas, deep and dangerous waters; and how will you escape? You'll be in a pretty pickle once you go to them . . . It's so crowded at your brother-in-law's, all those people living on top of one another in a poky house, each voicing his own opinions, each wanting his own way, how will you get away from them . . . Three of your nephews are grown men already, only the fourth is still a minor; soon they will be getting married and willy-nilly you'll be at the mercy of their wives. There are girls in the family too . . . The house is bursting at the seams with people . . . Even now there isn't room for all of them. Naturally, some will want to move in here. Then gradually they'll take over your land — to cultivate it for you, they will say, but then just try to get them out! I'm not saying that you shouldn't go to them, of course not, but . . . Listen, Thomas, wouldn't it perhaps be better to wait and see how things pan out before deciding? Rather than rushing in headlong, wham-bang! All in good time, wouldn't you say?'

And as he went on talking like this, he kept blinking his little eyes and smiling.

'I've been thinking about it too . . . I might have a rough time over there . . .'

'Don't do anything too hastily!'

'Don't worry . . . Let me sort things out . . . The only trouble is, my seedlings all need hoeing, my tobacco needs picking, stringing up to dry and rolling . . . No end of tasks requiring labour, and labour costs money. And as you can imagine, at present I don't have any. Where would it come from? My old woman's illness has put back all my plans. For some days now I've been wanting to hire a couple of hard-working girls, but how could I leave the house? Was I supposed to lock her up in there alone? So you see, if my nephews and nieces were around my chores would already have been seen to.'

'Don't you worry . . . Tomorrow, tomorrow I'll send my wife and sister-in-law, my son and daughter and my niece to do those outdoor jobs for you . . . If you'd mentioned it earlier they'd all have been done by now, but today's already half over and we might not get round to it tomorrow either, because as you say she's going to die this evening . . . right? So let's wait until the following day perhaps . . . You know what a feisty woman my sister-in-law is, Thomas, she simply eats the fields up! There's not a man able to keep pace with her.'

'A real woman!' replied Thomas, his eyes sparkling.

Argyris looked at him with his lively little eyes, smiled and shook his head. But then suddenly he became dejected as he recalled how death kept encroaching on their neighbourhood, and reflected that he himself was a sick man and death would no doubt soon ascend the hill again, this time for him. The thought of death always made him tremble. 'So she's dying? Really dying?' he asked gloomily. 'And probably tonight, you say? At what hour, who can tell!'

'Yes . . .' Thomas replied impatiently, as if fearful that by some magic power Argyris's words might prolong her life. 'Yes, and it's high time she went. Better for her too, lying there in agony poor woman, as if she were paying for the most heinous crimes! . . . Better for us as well! . . . The Catholic priests have the right idea! . . . People say, and no doubt it's true, that they delay absolution to the very last minute. Absolution? . . . Damnation more like! And if the sick man lingers once he's been absolved, to make sure he won't recover and live on, the priest grips him by the throat and finishes him off. To my mind, they are right to do so, they save mankind a lot of suffering.'

'Ah, what is man?' Argyris went on wistfully. 'Like the grass on the plane... green today, dried up tomorrow in the wake of the Grim Reaper. We toil and moil here in this life, as if we were on earth for ever, and forget that we are only passing through!... Crimes, robberies, injustices, we commit them all... Yet life's so sweet and death frightens us so much... It terrifies us... Then suddenly the summons comes and we must heed it, whether we will or not. We must leave this fair world and all its blessings, whether we will or not, and who knows what awaits us in the next. All very disturbing!... And mysterious!...'

Thomas shrugged.

'I'll go and see how the old woman's getting on,' he said. 'I've been away some time.'

'Think about everything I've said!' Argyris shouted after him as he went out.

'Don't you worry,' he replied.

# III

It was the dead of night. The whole village was asleep and only in Thomas's house was anyone astir at that late hour. A grimy oil-lamp was hanging from a nail above the bed, its red flame licking up the flaking wall and blackening it steadily as it struggled to dispel the darkness. The fire in the hearth had gone out and the two thick logs lying in the ashes looked like corpses. Everything was pitch black inside the house. The glistening flue was black right up to the rafters, the crumbling plastered walls, their masonry showing through, were black with grime, the well-trodden earth floor was black, the beams were blackened by centuries of smoke, even the icon above the bed was black. At that hour the very air seemed black, like fine dense soot pervading the whole house and obscuring the light emitted by the oil-lamp. And the darkness reeked of smoke, spilled wine, sheep, goats and another nauseating stench which emanated from the bed.

The lamp shone down upon it. It was supported by two high wooden trestles and was filthy. From beneath the tattered greasy quilt and dirty sheets an emaciated wrinkled face protruded, the aged face of Thomas's wife battling for her life. Now and then a faint inarticulate groan came from her pale and withered lips. Her eyes in their hollow unwashed sockets were closed, her long pale nose was thin as a blade and diaphanous, the nostrils quivering slightly, and her whole ugly wrinkled little face was glistening with sweat. Her unkempt white hair had escaped her grubby headband and fallen about her ears, the odd strand sticking to her hollow cheeks and fleshless brow, and her Adam's apple stood out sharply, as if carved in wood, and now and then moved up and down. Her wrinkled bony hands, aged by work and sickness, plucked incessantly at the soiled bedding, or reached up to her forehead as if in search of something and then fell back to her side. Every so often her whole body would be convulsed with fear and she would groan aloud.

Her husband came over to the bed and stood looking down at her.

'I doubt she'll last the night!' he muttered shaking his head.

A second old woman, Thomas's sister, who was sitting huddled in the dark beside the chilly hearth, her head against the wall and occasionally nodding off, replied drowsily, 'Who knows . . .'

On the bed the dying woman gave a start, groaned and half opened one frightened eye, moving her lips as if to speak and struggling in vain to swallow her saliva.

'She must be thirsty . . .' Thomas said.

His sister rose from her stool, yawned, rubbed her eyes and shuffled over to a table that in the dark was barely visible at the foot of the bed.

'Shouldn't we give her some cordial?' she suggested in a nasal voice.

'Cordial!' laughed Thomas. 'That's all she needs right now! She's at death's door already, can't you see? You'd think God would put her out of her misery quickly; what good is life to her like this, why prolong her suffering? Just moisten her parched lips a little and mind she doesn't choke . . .'

The invalid gave another start, as if she had understood, and blinked an eye.

Thomas's sister fetched a cup of water and a wooden spoon and moistened the dying woman's lips. Then sitting on the bed with the cup in one hand and the spoon in the other, she gazed thoughtfully at the pale face of the woman destined shortly to depart this world. Finally, shaking her head sadly, she reflected, 'Poor Angela . . . now you too are leaving, like so many before you . . . You were a good woman, despite your quirks and crotchets. At least you're departing well prepared. You've confessed and had communion. And your husband bears you no ill will, since you always honoured and respected him! A shame you didn't bear the poor man any children . . . Who's going to look after him in his old age? True, he has my children, but nephews and nieces are never quite the same.* Whereas he took care of all your needs, in life and death alike . . .'

Terror again convulsed the whole body of the dying woman. Her eyes filled with tears and in a faint voice she whispered, 'Am I dy . . .'

A groan of anguish followed.

'Her heart will give out any minute,' whispered the other woman with bated breath.

Brother and sister stood waiting for the end to come at any moment. Everywhere silence reigned — a silence both of them could hear, like a humming in the ears. The lamp spluttered, grew dim and began to smoke, but then revived, its red flame dancing.

A dog could be heard barking in the distance. In Thomas's shed or perhaps Argyris's stable a rat dislodged some rubble as it scurried off, then silence again descended, a quiet that continued to be audible.

'Hasn't she gone yet?' Thomas exclaimed impatiently.

'Not yet . . .' replied his sister. 'God wants to try her in this life so that she may shortly find the gates of heaven open.'

Tears started to the dying woman's eyes again.

'She can hear us . . .' Thomas said.

'Yes, she can!' replied his sister indifferently. 'Whether she wants to or not, she's going to die . . .'

This seemed to galvanize the dying woman: her hands twitched, she opened her bleary eyes in terror and stared at Thomas and his sister, then, as if her strength were suddenly reviving, she flung her exhausted head from side to side, breathed in a couple of times, swallowed painfully and said, 'I can't bear it! I can't bear it! . . . Agh! . . . Agh! . . .' Then she struggled to raise herself and sit up in bed, but to no avail. 'I can't bear it! Agh! . . . Agh! . . .' she repeated, sweating.

'Soon you will be at peace for ever,' said the other old woman nodding gravely. 'Yes, it won't be long now! . . .' And she held her hand to prevent her injuring herself.

'In the next world there will be neither pain nor sorrow! You'll be departing very soon . . .'

'I can't bear it, I can't bear it!' reiterated the sick woman feebly, falling back against the pillow as if in a faint.

'Has she died?' her husband asked.

'No,' replied his sister.

A deathly silence again descended. Both of them watched every laboured breath the dying woman drew, every twitch of her parched lips, every contraction of her throat, every slight flutter of her eyelids, both expecting her to expire at any moment. For a brief interval the stillness of the night erupted into life. In some distant neighbourhood a cock crowed once, twice, three times and then fell silent.* A moment later two, then three, then many more cocks answered, their cries drawing ever nearer, resounding from one neighbourhood to the next across the village, until finally their own neighbourhood cock sang out loud and clear, followed even more loudly and melodiously by the cock inside Argyris's barn. Then one by one the birds close by fell silent and the more distant crowing could be heard again, and soon quiet reigned once more .

'The first cock-crow . . .' said Thomas without thinking.

The dying woman opened her eyes and saw her husband standing next to her. She looked him in the eye for several seconds and then said in a faint hoarse voice, 'Hangman Thomas, you've put me in the ground! . . .'

On hearing his nickname, Thomas immediately became irate and looked fiercely about the room, conscious of his throat constricting and the blood surging to his head, then unable to control himself he raised his fist, took a step back and glaring at her said, 'Even now, confound it, even now, dying in your own shit, you must provoke me! A curse upon the soul you'll be delivering to the Devil . . .'

'Get out!' shouted his sister in alarm. 'How dare you mention the Evil One by name, just as she's about to give up the ghost! He's sure to be lurking nearby to snatch her sinful soul, if he gets half a chance . . . And you invoke him? Don't you see you're doing him a favour . . . I spit on him!'* And she spat.

The eyes of the dying woman clouded over.

'Hangman Thomas . . .' she repeated under her breath.

He again became irate and grinding his teeth raised his fist to strike her, but then suddenly thinking better of it he rushed over to the door and flung it open.

'When you reach your destination,' he said, 'wherever that may be, tell your father and your mother that I curse them to this day . . .'

Then he turned to go.

'Where are you off to?' asked his sister, getting off the bed and seizing him by the arm. 'I'm not staying here alone, I'm too afraid . . . How can you take offence at her, poor Thomas? She's no longer aware of what she's saying, she can't even *hear* you now . . .'

'Agh!' growled Thomas through clenched teeth.

'Hangman Thomas . . .' whispered the invalid again from the bed.

The other old woman quickly sealed her mouth.

'My curse upo-o-o-n you, and upon your fa-a-a-ther, and upon your mo-o-o-ther,' chanted Thomas, raising his voice to a singsong and beating time with his foot.

He stood in the doorway and gazed up at the stars. He could only see a few, as all but a small patch of sky was obscured by the adjacent hillside with its tall cypresses and olive trees which seemed strangely diminished at that hour, mere shadowy clumps in the pale starlight. He stood there for some time. Not a sound came from within the house now. He waited, listening intently, expecting his sister to announce the end at any moment. After waiting for some time, he asked impatiently, 'Is she dead yet?'

'Not yet,' replied his sister. 'It won't be long now . . .'

'What time can it be?' he asked himself fretfully and again looked at the stars. 'Even the cocks can sometimes be mistaken,' he murmured. 'Occasionally they crow a good three hours before dawn . . .'

He didn't recognize the stars he could see, and the ones he knew were out of sight. But he had suddenly calmed down and inhaled the cool clear night air deep into his lungs. Hundreds of frogs were croaking in the ditches, now and then lapsing into collective silence, while from among the trees came the sound of crickets chirping.

'What time can it be?' he wondered again. Suddenly he became angry and resentful, why he could not tell, and muttered irritably, 'Even the stars are hidden from us by the people's wretched olive trees and the orchards of the landlord, God damn his father!'

Then suddenly he regretted cursing him and asked himself, 'Why did I curse the good gentleman, and at a time like this!' He remembered the handsome old noble with his gracious air, his snow-white beard, his courteous manners, his guileless smile and his innocent sympathetic gaze. 'At a time like this . . .' he continued. 'Soon Angela will meet him in the next world, and if she overheard me is bound to tell him . . . But there of course she'll be the mistress and the nobleman the slave . . . That's what the Gospel says . . .'

He went outside, walked round the house and stood in the garden for a while, trying to make out whether the morning star had risen in the East and whether he could guess the position of the Pleiades from the configuration of the other stars, now that his old eyes could no longer see the smaller ones.

'Daybreak is still three hours away,' he said to himself finally as he re-entered the house. 'Three whole hours to go.'

He looked about. The sick woman lying on the bed was still breathing and his sister had resumed her seat by the hearth and had nodded off. He took a few rolled leaves of tobacco and a pocket-knife out of his sash, sat down on the end of one of the trestles supporting the bed, pushing back the bedding from a plank, and under the red light from the lamp proceeded to crush the tobacco between finger and thumb and chop it fine. This done, he carefully gathered it into his palm and stashed it away in his jacket pocket. Then from the same pocket he produced a cigarette paper and, using the slivers of tobacco remaining on the plank, rolled himself a thick drooping cigarette, put it in his mouth, got up and lit it at the lamp. Finally, after taking a few puffs and glancing again at the sick woman, he sat down by the hearth opposite his sister and, resting his head in his hand, proceeded to smoke.

Meanwhile the dying woman had started talking to herself deliriously. She rambled on, addressing her father, her mother and her dead siblings. Imagining she was still a little child, she would call out to their horse which had died some twenty years ago, and every so often she would groan or weep. Thomas listened to her with indifference.

Just then she had opened her eyes and was raving on again: 'A star! Oh look, a star! . . . It's shining through the tiles . . . That's where the roof will leak, of course . . . It's way up there in the sky, but I can see it . . . It's not moving . . . It's standing still . . . Why isn't it moving with the others? Mother, where are you? . . . Why, Mother, oh why did Thomas turn you out? So that you couldn't change my bed-sheets either and the worms would eat me alive before I descend into the grave . . . I'm still a little girl, a poor little thing; how can I escape this prison-house of his? . . . Why are so many moths flitting round the candle flame? . . . They're trying to put it out, yes, they're going to put it out, there it goes! . . . But the flame has singed their wings! . . . Oh, all these black spiders nibbling my eyes, oh, I'm so afraid, oh, oh! My head is coming off . . . So you're going to take it from me and roll it all the way down the hill onto the beach, eh? Pitiless fate . . . Is there no one here beside me? Oh, oh!'

The red flame of the lamp bobbed up and down, smoking and spluttering occasionally as a ball of soot lodged in the wick like a glowing coal and dimmed the light. And each time the lamp flared up it would die down further, as if about to fizzle out; and then revive, as if it too were reluctant to expire. And Thomas, still smoking his cigarette, kept telling himself he should get up and tend the lamp but then putting it off, persuading himself the light would last a little longer, as if fearful lest by adding oil he might prolong the dying woman's life; and meanwhile his eyes grew heavier, closing agreeably between each puff.

The dying woman would fall silent for a few minutes and then ramble on again; the lamp went on flickering as the air eddied round the charred wick, then finally guttered, ready to go out beside the life expiring next to it. The cigarette fell from Thomas's lips and his head fell back against the wall. He was fast asleep and snoring . . .

He was wakened by his sister, shaking him vigorously.

It was still dark inside the house, save for a faint gleam coming from a chink.

'Not a sound from her,' she said. 'She must have passed away.'

'Dawn,' said Thomas looking at the rafters. 'Daybreak at last.'

He stood up in the dark, stretching and yawning noisily.

'Let in some light . . .' said his sister.

He did not reply but, still half asleep, went across and opened the shutters.

The eastern sky was aglow above the dark hills which obscured the horizon. A few high clouds were turning a delicate pale pink. The birds were starting to twitter in the trees. The village cocks were crowing again from neighbourhood to neighbourhood. Now and then footsteps echoed down the village street. Somewhere close by a door opened and someone coughed; in some other house people were already talking . . .

But inside Thomas's house there was still almost no light. Only the small square of the window stood out in the prevailing gloom, nothing else could be discerned, not even someone moving. Thomas's sister meanwhile had approached the bed and, groping for Angela's hand, sighed and said, 'She's stone cold . . . God have mercy on her . . . She has passed away.'

And a moment later she continued, 'Light the lamp. I'll go and fetch the dresser to prepare the corpse. I can't do it on my own.'

She found her way to the door and was about to go out when she paused a moment and added softly as if to avoid being overheard, 'In the meantime, hide anything you need to hide. Look, it's getting light. Her heirs will be upon us soon and they'll take anything that belonged to her . . .* Though I don't see why they should when they haven't lifted a finger to help, not even at the end! . . .'

'Don't you worry,' he said, reaching for the lamp and taking it down from the wall. 'She had a will drawn up in my favour by the notary, so no one else gets anything.'

Meanwhile he had replenished the lamp and, turning his back on the corpse to avoid being suddenly confronted with it in the light, he struck a match.

'No one else gets anything,' he repeated cunningly, aware that his sister's remarks were aimed at obtaining his wife's clothing for her daughters.

By this time the lamp was burning brightly. Everything was in place exactly as before, except that no groans or mutterings were coming from the bed.

The woman left and Thomas shook his head wryly as he watched her go. Then, still avoiding looking at the corpse so close to him, he crossed to the window, rolled himself another thick drooping cigarette and leaned out, his elbows resting on the sill. He felt neither sorrow nor distress at Angela's demise, but nor did he rejoice.

All he knew was that her death would change his life completely. Would it be for the better or the worse? Who could tell? One thing was certain, that the old woman's illness had been a long one, the more so in their tiny house and since it was bound to end in death. Now she too had been set free. Both of them had suffered. Such were his thoughts and yet he still didn't dare look at the corpse, picturing it with vague dread stretched out on the bed, its eyes half open, its mouth gaping and its hair unkempt in all the ugliness of old age.

Outside, the whole of the eastern sky had now grown lighter. A myriad birds were singing in the branches. The village was awake. Doors and windows were opening on all sides. People's voices could be heard — women feeding their chickens, coaxing their flocks or scolding their children, men goading their horses up the road or laughing in the village stores, children throwing tantrums. The day had at last begun. Any minute now the sun would rise. Thomas no longer feared his wife's ghost might creep up on him behind his back, but he couldn't help brooding over their past life together, an entire lifetime ... And now she was in the next world, a better world than this no doubt, but one he was not ready for just yet and would prefer never to experience; but when at last he did enter it and encountered his dead wife again, perhaps her only acknowledgement would be: 'Haven't we met somewhere before? ...'\*

For the time being however she was lying stretched out lifeless on the bed. Where would he sleep tonight, in the very house where she had just expired? He still had not brought himself to look at her. Oh, he'd look at her eventually, of course he would. But all in good time.

First let the sun come up.

Suddenly in the garden his donkey started braying.* 'Poor beast,' he thought, 'if I don't put out some fodder, it will go hungry, tied up there all day...' He promptly forgot everything else and brusquely turned toward the door, and it was then that he accidentally set eyes on the corpse for the first time. His aged spouse had expired with her head turned to the wall; her open mouth was cavernous and twisted, her glazed eyes wide and staring; her face was grey and her whole expression bore witness to her terrible ordeal.

'Ah!' sighed Thomas and crossed himself, before leaning over and kissing her pale fleshless brow.

Then he covered her face, turning up the end of the soiled sheet, and made for the door. Suddenly it occurred to him that his sister and the dresser would be opening the trunk, as they had to dress the corpse, and would be able to steal anything they fancied from her trousseau. So returning to the bed he put his hand under the bedclothes, took the keys from the dead woman's belt, opened the trunk himself and after selecting the white garments they would need from among the pile of clothes, relocked the trunk and pocketed the key. Then looking round to make sure everything was in order, he put the two thick plates and wooden spoons away, poured the last of her medicine out of the window and replaced the phial on the shelf, then went out to feed the donkey.

Almost at once however he returned accompanied by his sister and the elderly dresser, a strong woman with an ugly face, and stationed himself beside the door to watch.

The two old women at once set about their thankless task. They lifted the dead woman and immediately a nauseating stench pervaded the whole house, so revolting indeed that despite themselves all three of them were obliged to hold their noses.

Then the women started to undress her. And with every movement they made, the dead woman's head lolled from side to side, jerking forward or falling back, and occasionally a groan issued from the corpse's chest. Suddenly the two women let go of her, tugging their cheeks in horror.

'Oh, oh, the poor thing!' they cried.

'What's wrong?' asked Thomas.

'Oh, oh, Thomas...' said the dresser, 'you let the worms eat her alive!'

'Me?' said Thomas.

'That's why she stank so,' groaned his sister.

Thomas spat on the ground in utter revulsion and went out to feed the donkey. He remained in the garden for a long while. When he finally returned, the corpse had been prepared and now lay on a spotless white sheet, meticulously groomed and clad in white. Sprinkled on the sheets and dress were lemon leaves and sprigs of some other plant that smelt of roses. Just then the dresser bent down and whispered thrice into the dead woman's ear, 'Hold tight, Angela, don't disgrace your family!'

'What's she saying to her?' Thomas asked his sister.

'It's a charm,' she replied, 'to prevent her nest of lice from bursting.'

# IV

It was later that morning. Thomas was sitting on the crumbling stone steps to his front door, which now stood open, silently smoking a thick drooping cigarette. Beside him stood the tall stout pallid figure of Argyris, leaning on a thick stick clasped in one hand behind his back and looking about, while also keeping an eye on what was going on inside the house.

It was crowded with people. Andreas and Amalia were sitting outside the kitchen door, laughing, teasing and pinching one another. Maria's two little boys were playing in the mud in the yard, while Olga and Chrysanthi's daughter Aglaïa were coaxing the sheep out to take them down into the valley.

Inside Thomas's house, laid out on the bed, was his wife's corpse, small, ugly, with greyish hollow cheeks and mouth awry and dressed entirely in white. Four elderly solemn-faced women were standing round the bed contemplating the deceased and occasionally shaking their heads sadly.

Scurrying restlessly to and fro over the shroud and even onto the headscarf was a swarm of lice like so many white ants; by the bedside stood a lighted candle; the blackened icon had been placed upon the corpse. The house smelled of incense and spilled wine; no one wept.

'Such a good neighbour!' Chrysanthi was saying, her head wobbling. 'And now we've lost her... May God have mercy on her! May God have mercy on you, Angela!'

'Such a good woman... Such a good housewife,' lamented Thomas's sister, the one who had tended to her needs. 'So kind, so devoted to her husband...'

'There were five of us originally,' another bent little old woman was saying. 'Now I'm alone in the world; fate has cut down all the others. It's been years since my three unmarried sisters passed away, alas... Yes, I was the only daughter of my father to have children, long may they live... Angela, poor thing, was barren... Our mother let Thomas marry her without informing him. She was wrong to do so, because Angela paid dearly for it. Her husband was quite justified... He married to have children. Now, Angela, you are finally at peace. May

God have mercy on you!'

She nodded her head sadly.

'Ah well!' said the dresser, 'the same fate awaits us all! So many have now passed through my hands! And what does any man take with him? Only his wickedness or his good deeds. Whatever we say about this woman, others will say about us tomorrow when we're six feet under! If people bore death in mind, they would never do anything wicked...'

Squatting on a thick log by the cold hearth was Yannis, fat, ruddy, his eyes half closed, ready as ever for a chat; and standing next to him were three young lads, the nephews of Thomas and the deceased.

Maria was sitting on the black chest at the foot of the bed, her feet dangling, and next to her was her sister, the priest's wife, a proud and lively middle-aged woman with a wrinkled face and not many teeth. The two of them were discussing their affairs. Their remarks were so elliptical that a stranger would have had difficulty following them.

'About the division,' whispered Maria, 'we've discussed it with Argyris.'

'With Argyris!' said the priest's wife, glancing at her sister fiercely. 'D'you mind telling me why Argyris should be meddling in our affairs? Has living with them made you stupid too?'

'You know very well,' she replied tossing her head resentfully, 'that cold-hearted fellow rules the roost with us! My husband doesn't want to divide things with his brother, because, he says, our affairs are running smoothly as they are, and that's true enough. Every day that sickly Argyris makes some new acquisition. My husband works hard, poor man, but if he were in charge, everything would slip through his fingers. He's a bit of a spendthrift, is my Yannis, and he knows it, which is why he's afraid to strike out on his own; he's worried we might starve, he says; you know my Yannis, he's a treasure!'

'And is he also that hesitant in bed with you?' asked the priest's wife teasingly.

'Goodness... Is that all you ever think about, and you married to the Reverend! Have you no respect for the deceased? Tut, tut!'

And she suppressed a giggle.

'Of course,' said the priest's wife with a knowing little nod, 'Lord Argyris is interested in the house, because he doesn't want to share his patrimonial home with you... A big fat tub of lard like him, you see, can't live in half a house. He's rotten to the core...'

'That's not the reason; he says you'll give us land in compensation.'

'I'll discuss it with my husband . . .' replied her sister and gazing at the corpse she heaved a sigh.

Then shaking her head sadly she continued, 'Soon the priests will be here to take her away, alas . . . and they'll bury her beneath the earth, where all of us end up . . .'

'All of us!' Maria sighed as well.

'It won't be long now . . .' said the dead woman's sister pensively, as if these last remarks had frightened her.

Then, as she looked about, the chest caught her eye and she called out, 'Thomas!'

'What is it?' he replied from where he was sitting on the doorstep, looking round into the room and blowing a thick cloud of smoke from his mouth.

The old woman slowly approached him, stooping as she shuffled to the door.

'Thomas,' she said, 'where are the keys to the chest?'

Thomas was on his feet at once and coming up the steps into the room he looked her fiercely in the eye and, slapping his thick jacket pocket, said, 'They're here, in here!'

'Don't be offended,' wheedled the old woman 'but as you know, the chattels of the dear departed now belong to us, everything she owned, though we won't make a fuss if one or two items she brought you should be missing. The lads have come to cart it all away.'

'Ah yes, her heirs,' said Thomas with a sneer.

'It's not as if they're strangers . . .' said the old woman gently. 'They're her own flesh and blood . . . And as she had no children, they will . . .'

'A pile of shit is all she left you . . .' Thomas interrupted her angrily.

'Shameless, insolent man . . .' she scolded him sighing, 'how's that for delicacy . . . He's no respect even for her corpse, the apostate. Who knows how he treated her . . . He's the one who put her in the ground, poor woman . . . But mark my word, Thomas, you'll come to a bad end!'

Then after a pause she gripped her gullet with one hand and hissed, 'Hangman by name, hangman by nature . . .'

'Hangman . . . hangman . . .' he replied flushing red at once, unable to control himself. 'Ah, if only I were one and could execute your children! My name is Thomas, Thomas Kapsalis; you know full well I am no hangman! . . . Well, I like that, she turns up with her children like an heiress and starts abusing me . . .'

And with shoulders hunched, he shook his finger in the air.

'That's right, that's right . . . instead of first asking the notary what's in the will . . .'

Then suddenly he calmed down and, resuming his seat on the steps, he continued in his most caressing voice, 'My Angela's poor father, may God forgive him, was a cuckold, a natural cuckold! I, for one, planted a fine pair of horns right here in the middle of his forehead! Mmm! My poor Angela fell in love with me, you see! We won't mention the triumphs of your other sister . . . with your late cousin, with the landlord, and just about everybody else . . . We'd be here all night! And what about your two unmarried sisters, now deceased? Their name is still being dragged through the mud in society today. How could anyone forget them! They were great fun as well! Mmm! Mmm!'

And he brought his right forefinger and thumb together and wagged them up and down appreciatively.

'And further back, what about all your great-aunts and ancestors of old? A long line of them, poor things! But then that's only natural. Where do apples fall? Underneath the apple tree . . .* Some a little closer, some a little further off, but always underneath, always! . . .'

Inside the room they were barely able to contain their laughter. Pale and beside herself with fury, the deceased woman's sister was at a loss as to what to do next. She looked round from face to face, as if seeking a defender, then signalling to her sons beside the hearth to rise, she went over to her sister's corpse, crossed herself, bent and kissed the icon, then overcoming her revulsion brushed the dead woman's forehead with her lips and hurriedly left the house. Her sons followed her out.

'You're a shameless fellow, Hangman Thomas,' she said angrily, spitting on the ground as she passed by him.

He began cursing her again in the same caressing tone, then finally he said, 'Wait a moment, woman, bless your eyes . . . Here comes the notary, ask him whether she left anything to you.'

He pointed down the road leading into the village.

And sure enough, quite a crowd was now coming up the hill. Leading the way were four young men smartly dressed in European clothes* carrying the bier, holding it casually with one hand and laughing and joking amongst themselves. Not far behind them came the three village priests in their soft cruciform caps and their threadbare cassocks, to which time had lent a greenish sheen, accompanied by a fourth man, the notary, father of Maria and the priest's wife, a tall stooping elderly gentleman with an ancient patrician boater and a stout stick. He too was wearing European clothes. His old jacket had once been brown but was now frayed and patched at the elbows with a greenish material, evidently from one of his son-in-law's old cassocks, and his crumpled trousers were likewise extensively patched around the knees. He was an extremely frail old man with dry transparent skin and cheeks made rosy by a fine network of subcutaneous veins, and a long straight nose with quivering nostrils, the tip of which was also red. His eye-sockets with their dark, still lively eyes were hollow, as were his bony temples and his withered cheeks, and he had a trim white moustache above his thin red lips.

The three priests were engaged in serious lofty conversation with the notary, raising their voices and gesturing emphatically as they used the occasion to explore the great and terrifying mystery of death.

After them came several children, most of them barefoot and in short sleeves, laughing and chattering amongst themselves. One was carrying the silver censer, another the silver cross, its pole detached and tucked under his arm, while still other children were in charge of the priests' brightly coloured vestments, all turned inside out* and folded neatly, and of the vessels containing holy water. They were followed by about twenty villagers coming up the hill with them to join in the funeral procession.

On seeing the crowd, the deceased woman's sister stepped aside and waited to avoid having to pass among the men advancing up the narrow road.

By now the priests and the notary had reached Thomas's door with the bier and as the four men were taking it inside, Thomas without so much as a greeting shouted, 'Your Honour, explain things to this woman — tell her whether or not she has any claims here, because I can't get her off my back; she insists that she's the heir and won't take no for an answer! . . .'

And in his faint high-pitched tremulous voice, which issued like a gentle breeze from his thin rosy lips, while his whole face seemed to smile — his habitual expression even when he was depressed or angry — the notary replied, 'Yes, yes, I myself drew up her will last year, this time last year . . . Thomas, Thomas is the sole beneficiary and heir to all her worldly goods! That's right . . .'

'You see?' said Thomas, 'he's made my claim rock solid, fit to withstand the stiffest southerly!'

By now the priests outside the door had donned their stoles and one was entering the house. The corpse had already been placed on the narrow black bier and the four smartly dressed young men were in place ready to raise it. The priests coughed, murmured blessings and scattered incense as they gathered round the corpse, then each said a prayer for the departed, while the men and women inside the house crossed themselves repeatedly and sighed. Thomas had remained outside and the villagers who had arrived with the priests shook hands with him with one hand, while doffing their straw hats with the other. The boy carrying the cross attached it to its pole, while the one in charge of the censer ran round to Argyris's kitchen and filled it with live coals before bringing it into the house.

Now the customary chanting began, the men standing with heads bared. Everybody crossed themselves and murmured, 'God have mercy on her!' Moments later the priests re-emerged and lined up outside three abreast behind the cross, each with a thick unlighted candle in his left hand and a thin lighted one in his right. The boy with the censer ran and gave it to the tall priest in the middle and then kissed his hand.

For a minute or two they all waited expectantly, then finally the bier with its light burden emerged from the door on the shoulders of the four bearers, bobbing up and down as they descended the rough path.

'Alleluia! Alleluia! Alleluia!' the three priests began intoning and the funeral procession got under way.

The crowd waited a moment longer to let Thomas be the first to follow. Turning and seeing the priests already setting off down the hill with the corpse, he became agitated and as if acting spontaneously shouted irritably into the house, 'Hurry up now, ladies, God bless us! I want to lock up, for heaven's sake; who are you hoping to console in here! . . . '

The women looked at one another undecided for a moment, then finally one of them made a move and they all trooped out after her. As they emerged each shook hands with the old man, who was getting more and more impatient, wishing him 'Long life!'

He shook their hands with one hand while holding the door open by its huge key with the other.

Last to emerge was his own sister, who also expressed her condolences and pausing beside him said plaintively, 'I nursed her for so many days, Thomas, how can you turn me out like this? At least let me have her clothes! . . .'

Thomas glared at her angrily.

'Allow me to lock up now, will you,' he said, 'they've started off already, can't you see? Is this the moment? Perhaps if you come again another time . . .'

And he cursed under his breath.

His elderly sister slowly shuffled past him, her face averted, and having seen her out, the old man hastily slammed and locked the door, grumbling as he did so; then he hurried off to catch up with the funeral procession, by now disappearing down the hill. The crowd followed him in silence.

# V

Summer was now already half over and it was late one afternoon. A cool north wind was blowing and there was not a single cloud in the clear blue sky. The sea beyond looked choppy and the distant mountains, bathed in evening light, were a pale yellow. Everywhere the dry grass rustled in the breeze. The cypresses brushed against each other, their tips dipping now and then toward the earth.

Thomas was sitting alone on his crumbling stone doorstep in the cool. He had grown a full white beard, as he was still officially in mourning for his wife, and as he sat there he worked away, carving a distaff with his curved chisel. After first trimming the straight olive sprig, he had carved five bands around its upper end, three raised, two incised, and was now decorating the panels between them with crosshatching, using the tip of his chisel to remove the little chips of wood. As he worked, he chanted monotonously:

> *Beautiful a beauty is, five or ten times over,*
> *But best of all's a woman with her lover.**

And he went on repeating this same couplet again and again.

He had been sitting there for quite a while. It was now about the time that the village women would be going to the well. Soon a group of them appeared on the crest of the hill.

They were descending from a remote quarter of the village to join the road that ran past Thomas's door, laughing and chattering loudly as they came. They were all carrying their empty pitchers sideways on their shoulders — most of them unmarried girls, a few young wives and one old crone who appeared to be the ringleader.

'The upper villagers!' said Thomas to himself. 'Pandemonium again! I'd forgotten they'd be coming by as usual this evening.' His first impulse on hearing their cries was to get up and go inside at once, but he refrained from doing so as he did not want to appear to be avoiding them. 'Once I start that,' he reflected, 'they'll have me for breakfast. And then there'll be no end of it!' So he went on singing and working away, pretending not to notice them:

> *Beautiful a beauty is, five or ten times over,*

*But best of all's a woman with her lover.*

The women had halted for a moment and one young girl still in her teens, a dark ugly little creature in bare feet, suddenly exclaimed, 'Look girls! It's Hangman Thomas!... Down there!'

And she burst out laughing, pointing with her finger to where he was sitting. At once the others started laughing too.

'Hush, girls, shame on you... Hush, he's hardly going to take it as a joke...' said the old crone in a nasal voice and chuckled. She was an unkempt red-faced woman in bare feet, wearing an ancient man's jacket with torn pockets which was far too big for her. 'Shame on you, he'll only swear at us! An elderly gentleman like him! Behave yourselves... Oh, there will be hell to pay today; I'm turning back...'

And she too laughed aloud.

They set off again together along the narrow path and came hurtling down the hill, laughing and skipping, towards the first few houses.

Then a tall young lass with lively eyes and regular features but a dusky complexion called out, trying to suppress a giggle, 'Good evening, Thomas; so you're carving distaffs?'

'Will you make me a present of one?' cried another girl.

'Shame on you, girls, it's a disgrace!' the old woman repeated in her nasal voice, smiling slyly beneath her dirty headscarf. 'Don't tease the gentleman... Come on now, girls... let's be on our way...'

'Now he's widowed, he'll be living like a monk, poor Hangman Thomas...' said a pretty young woman, chewing at her headscarf coyly.

At this all the women burst out laughing, while the old crone repeated, 'Let's be off now, girls...'

And nudging those next to her with her elbows she urged them on down the path.

So far the old man had not responded, but now he suddenly stopped singing and, flushing crimson, flung his distaff and chisel angrily aside, unable to control himself a moment longer, even though he knew it would only make things worse.

Then pretending to humour them, he replied good-naturedly, 'Widowed! Yes, that can't be helped, unless you take pity on me, pretty lass, and come and keep me company in bed... You won't come to any harm, my little chick... I can assure you... no harm at all...'

And as he said this he kept nodding reassuringly and smiling. But seeing them all laughing their heads off, he continued, 'Come in all of you, you too, madam, never mind your age, come in and I'll teach you a thing or two you couldn't learn at any high school, even in Athens . . . Yes, you don't want to be illiterate when you go to meet your bridegrooms . . . I may be old, but my words are sacred, more so than the Gospels . . .'

Then suddenly, unable to contain his rage, he bellowed, 'Curse the faith you all believe in!'

'Don't get angry, Thomas!' said the old woman civilly, while the others split their sides with laughter, 'and don't be so wicked . . . Forgive them, Thomas, they're just empty-headed girls, whereas you are an elderly and learned gent . . .'

'Temper, temper, Hangman Thomas!' another woman taunted him.

'Come my little Katerina, come inside' he replied, 'come and see if I am old, as you all say, come I'll show you . . . I've some raki and cognac put aside for you, drink all you want. My fig tree's full of figs, you can climb up and eat all you want . . . and I'll sit underneath and watch you, ha! ha! ha!'

And he kept nodding as he said this.

Suddenly Argyris appeared at his door, tall, stout and looking very pale. Angrily he rapped his thick stick on the stone step and the women immediately fell silent.

'You miserable fillies,' he spluttered in his high-pitched voice, 'have you no shame? What d'you think you're doing? How dare you come through other people's neighbourhoods making fun of people in their homes? I'll have you charged . . . You'll go to jail . . . You are an absolute disgrace . . . Do you think the old gentleman has no one to defend him? He's like a father to me, do you understand, now get out of my sight the pack of you! . . .'

Shamefacedly, the women ran off down the hill and a moment later had disappeared.

'Good on you!' said Thomas, smiling and sighing with relief.

'And as for you,' Argyris said severely, 'why can't you turn a deaf ear to them?'

'Whenever I hear that nickname — curse its inventor's father! — I don't know what comes over me! . . . I suddenly feel like crying and laughing at once, I rage and get so worked up I'm ready to tear myself apart, chop myself in two like any ant . . . I feel my own blood seething and rising to my head and then I just can't help answering back, be it in anger, or in jest, or through my tears! What can I do about it? And since my late lamented died, those young trollops have become more brazen! Before, it seems, they were afraid of her, but now my life is like this every evening! Every blessed evening . . . It's a miracle if a day goes by without them jeering at me. Ah, since my late lamented died, everything has been going wrong and my affairs have gone all haywire!'

And as he said this he rubbed his hands together anxiously.

'Without you,' he continued after a pause, 'I'd have starved to death by now; the bread you give me keeps me going . . .'

'Surely things aren't quite as bad as that . . .' said Argyris closing his little eyes and smiling. 'You're not exactly destitute! You're old and have no children, so what would it matter if you sold off the odd field?'

'Old? Old? . . . I'm not that old! My heart is like a child's and I still feel like one. By God! . . . All these years I never really noticed how I had become a man and then grown old. Even now when they tell me I am old, I still feel as if I'm the little boy that played in our neighbourhood the way your children do today! I feel my father might any minute call me in or my mother come out to feed me, but instead they are in the other world . . . The world of truth . . . I just can't believe I'm old already . . . Besides, I still have a good many years left in me. And I want to live. I enjoy life! I'm not consumed by malice, corroding my insides. I'm not a repressive person who's going to get consumption . . . Oh no . . . My anger subsides as swiftly as it rises. I calm down immediately and don't bear grudges. D'you understand what I'm saying? Remember the landlord? He was pushing ninety, God have mercy on him, and that priest who lives somewhere in the mountains, he's a hundred-and-four. So if I start selling things off now, in a year or two I'll have nothing left, and then what will become of me when old age really does set in? Besides, I'd be ashamed to sell my property . . . Woe to him who yields to temptation and starts touching it, it quickly vanishes like pollen . . . Puff!' and he blew on his open palm.

'You're right,' said Argyris slyly, again closing his eyes. 'To be secure in your old age you should find someone reliable and arrange an annuity with him, then you'll have so much a day for life and be free of worries. What do you think of the idea, eh? Don't you agree?'

And as Thomas remained silent, he went on: 'But that someone shouldn't be a nephew . . . of course not . . . nor a member of your family... What could you do about it if they defaulted on your payments, not because they didn't want to pay but because they didn't have the money. And it's true enough, they never have any... How should they? They're such a large family, a whole tribe of them... Any income that family receives is a mere drop in the bucket; all those children and old men and women are dependents... So don't look to your nephews. You must find someone who's not family, a complete outsider, but a pious man of course! You know what I mean, someone who believes in God!'

'This year,' said Thomas thoughtfully, 'I wouldn't have needed any help... But then as luck would have it she fell ill. All that time in bed, with doctors and medicaments to pay for, left me quite hard up. Such is life! I ended up selling her sheep as well as all the grain. I thought I'd plant potatoes, but the weeding was neglected and you can see the results for yourself. Over there...' And he pointed to a small heap of potatoes in the corner. 'That's the lot, not enough to plant again this year... And then as she lay dying, the rains came. It rained cats and dogs, I tell you! That was life, day after day... So my tobacco field remained fallow... I hadn't enough cash to hire labour in time to plant it when the sun came out, and your womenfolk had their own fields to attend to. So I had to handle all the work and instead of tobacco I ended up with fodder for everybody else's sheep, and now the field gets trampled all day long; it's a sight for sore eyes, a complete wasteland!... And so my affairs have gone all haywire!... I thought I might at least plant a bit of corn. Living alone, the yield would have provided me with bread for six or seven months. But now someone's gone and stolen it... God damn them!'

And with both hands he made an obscene gesture in the air.

'One of your relatives, no doubt!' said Argyris slyly. 'Who else?'

'I saw nothing and cannot bear witness... Whoever it was, confound him!'

'Think about that little matter I mentioned to you, though... Your olive groves and fields and the house, even with you in it, are worth a tidy sum, quite honestly... You should get five drachmas a day, a sweet fiver!* And then you can stay at home like a pasha and smoke your cigarettes... On a fiver a day you could even live in town... Think about it...'

'A fiver?' exclaimed Thomas staring at him in amazement.

'Certainly.'

'And where would one find such a person?'

'Well, we'll look into it . . .'

'Would you yourselves consider it?' asked Thomas with a crafty smile. 'My house is valuable to you, because you could join it to your own one day and build a regular seraglio.'

'Not really,' said Argyris indifferently 'What would we do with so many houses . . . As the old proverb says, "Land as far as the eye can see, a house no larger than need be" . . . Houses are always an expense. The villagers are all bankrupting themselves with their new building projects. They're stupid ignorant people. As soon as they've saved a couple of bob, they can't wait to build a mansion . . . That's the way they are . . . But let me have a word with my brother, it's his decision as much as mine, of course, and then we'll give you an answer.'

'Yannis?' smiled Thomas cunningly again, 'Yannis is your second self, of course, and you are his. But I've been having other ideas lately. I've been thinking I might remarry, fairly soon in fact, while my health holds out. I might even sire a child, who knows . . . but even if I didn't, I'd have a woman by my side, a servant free of charge.'

'And who would want you, my poor fellow?' replied Argyris quickly, disturbed by this development. 'That's right, who would want you? But joking aside, the years take their toll, you know. On the other hand, we might find some old crone for you, someone poor and looking for a place to rest her head, like lame Andriana say, or somebody like her . . . But then what would you have gained? You'd have made a hole in water . . . You'd again be saddled with a woman needing geriatric care . . . The same old story . . . The young ones won't look at you, of course . . . Except some desperate outcast, or someone who'd make you sign over everything to her. That might be a possibility. But just think what fate might have in store for you, if you did that . . . Hmm! . . . Hmm! . . .'

And both of them remained silent a few moments.

'Well I never, Thomas . . .' said Maria in her lovely voice, suddenly appearing, 'so you're contemplating marriage, eh . . . And with a young girl too . . . ha, ha. Virility's required for marriage, my poor Thomas . . . Didn't you see the way the village girls were crucifying you just now? And why? Because they're not afraid of you . . . And even the one you choose will make fun of you with all her friends, and in a year or two she'll have made your life a misery . . . Moo! Moo!'

And she moved her fist, with the index and little fingers extended, vigorously up and down above her forehead .

'Beware, poor Thomas,' she continued, 'lest they entangle you with someone and you regret it later. Then of course it will be too late. Even in our village there are bravos aplenty, bravos galore, believe you me . . .'

And she flourished her cupped right hand expressively.

'I was just considering it,' said Thomas shyly, 'that is, I've not decided yet . . .'

'You've no one else but us, poor Thomas,' Maria went on. 'Isn't that true? Our children are the only ones who care for you, you know . . . Any complaints? You can't have, by St Spyridon . . . They're the only children in the village who don't tease you. Come on, admit it. Ha, ha! I'd give them a good hiding if I ever heard them taunting you . . . And with us you've never gone without a thing, as we've got used to you and become quite fond of you. Be honest now . . . Ever since your Angela (may she rest in peace) departed, has there been anything you've gone without? Food or drink perhaps, or your washing, sewing, tidying, anything at all you've wanted? Tell me . . .'

'I too do what little jobs I can for you,' he replied proudly. 'I still have sturdy hands. I run errands for you with my donkey too. I mean, it's good of you to want me, but I earn my keep, you're not out of pocket . . .'

'I must just pop down to the village for a while,' Argyris suddenly declared, adjusting his fine boater. 'There's a small matter I must see to, so I have to rush. I'm negotiating for the purchase of a field; meanwhile you two have a little chat and sort things out. And if your sister drops by, Maria, make sure you don't do anything without consulting me, because your brother-in-law the priest's no fool. When you discuss things, I want to be there too . . .'

And with this he set off down the hill, smiling to himself.

Maria muttered under her breath, 'Scheme away, Argyris you consumptive, you won't live to enjoy your acquisitions, because you're rotten to the core! It's quite intolerable, can't we do anything without consulting you? What business have you meddling in our affairs, in my father's property, what's it got to do with you? My sister, the priest's wife, is quite right about you! Goodness!'

And with this she turned on her heel, entered Thomas's house and immediately set about making his bed. She now did this regularly every evening. Smiling, Thomas followed her, treading softly and stroking his white beard.

Maria looked at him and burst out laughing.

'While your strength holds out,' she said, 'you can manage well enough like this, but later on? Dark days lie ahead. Doom is written on the door!'

'The more I think about it,' he replied seriously, 'the more I feel I should find a companion, because . . .'

'Moo! Moo!' Maria teased him again, her two fingers raised above her forehead.

'I know,' he persisted, 'but how can I put it, I still need a woman! . . .'

'You're an old lecher!' she said and again laughed heartily.

'And what's more,' said Thomas looking at her lustfully, 'I don't need some innocent spring chicken . . . Just a buxom healthy woman — like your good self, for instance! . . . with the blood coursing through her lovely cheeks! . . .'

And as he said this he gradually drew closer.

Maria laughed without restraint again and giving him a side-long glance retorted, 'Ah Thomas, Thomas . . . you're very cunning, but I can see through you, you old rogue! So you want to play games, eh? Ha, ha, ha! But you know the old saying: "Is a stripling with the maid at play? Let them play and don't say nay! Is an old man with the maid at play? Then by and by he'll have his way!" My poor Thomas, I know you fancy me . . . Ha! Ha! Such things don't escape us women . . . But there's a fly in the ointment! . . .'

'Listen, Maria,' he said, his eyes sparkling. 'Listen . . . I'm not young but I have the heart of an eighteen-year-old lad. It's true . . .'

'Get away, you old goat!' Maria laughed again, wagging four fingers under her chin.

'I'll cut it off,' he replied, tugging at his beard. 'Tomorrow's Saturday and I'll have it shaved. Ah, gone are the days, Maria! You were a young lass in those days and I much older and already married; how I admired you whenever you came tripping through the village with the other women, carrying your pitcher and looking ravishing, yes ravishing, the fairest of them all! . . . Ah, if only I'd been widowed then, I'd have married you like a shot, but my cursed fate decided otherwise . . . And when you married Yannis I was overjoyed to hear you had become my neighbour, because I would be able to see you as often as I wanted, though of course I envied Yannis too . . . Now time has moved on, but when I recall all that I don't know what comes over me. I feel rejuvenated when I look at you, Maria, when you're near me, and I imagine how it would be if . . .'

As he was talking Thomas had quietly come up to her beside the bed, and now he suddenly put his powerful hands around her and drew her to him lustfully.

'Oh my darling! . . .' he murmured.

She gave him a fierce look at first, but was unable to restrain the laughter choking her, and with a giggle cried, 'Take your dirty hands off me! Let go of me this minute, you pathetic wretch . . . You're old and you revolt me . . . Come on, let me go, I tell you!'

And she spat on the ground. But Thomas still did not release her, and Maria started to get angry and with a look of fury stared directly into his face, which by now was flushed and inches from her own, but again she could not restrain her laughter. 'Go and shave your beard, you old goat,' she said. 'Your mouth's a field of stubble, you haven't any teeth and yet you want a woman! Ha, ha, ha! . . . Do you have anything to recommend you?'

And as she was saying this and laughing, she kept trying to escape, squirming, and wriggling her whole body.

'Let me go, I tell you, or I'll scream! This is beyond a joke! Leave me alone, Thomas! Don't you see, poor wretch, what a manly fellow shares my bed? You're old, you're ugly, you're revolting. I spit on you . . .'

And summoning all her strength, she managed to escape his grasp and reach the door.

'Ah, so that's the sort of man you are!' she went on shouting. 'Well, it's the last time I'll set foot inside your house; you won't see me in here again!'

He sighed and looked at her like a whipped dog, but made no reply. He was exhausted after their struggle and felt utterly dejected. Maria again laughed heartily, but then as if relenting she added gaily, 'But then again who knows . . . If I saw that you really loved me . . . Well, then perhaps my heart might yield . . . Otherwise why would I want you? You're hardly a better man than Yannis! But I'm not going to let you have your fun and laugh at me, no strings attached . . . Ah no, Thomas, that's not on!' And she reinforced this by shaking her head and finger simultaneously. 'I'll have to see first, I'll have to have proof of your devotion, and I mean real proof!... Otherwise, you're a man of property so off you go and marry, the sooner the better. You said you'd find a woman, didn't you! Or perhaps you think you can cheat me, Thomas, eh? Don't you know that I'm a wily bird? Perhaps you think you can install some other woman afterwards and the two of you then laugh at me together out of spite? Very clever, Thomas... but it won't wash with me... Oh, no!'

'I'll do anything you ask,' replied Thomas, throwing caution to the winds and clasping his hands. 'Only come to me, Maria, and everything is yours... Come, and afterwards treat me like your house-slave, feed me bread and water, take everything I own... But come, my darling... I'll make over everything to you; if you say so, I'll follow Glavostathis, who dabbled in black magic and signed his soul over to the Devil, keeping nothing but a teaspoon in his sash.* Oh, don't leave me! Have you no compassion?'

Maria however went on laughing. She found the besotted old man amusing and no longer felt afraid of him.

The door was just behind her.

'We'll have to see,' she told him 'it's all up to you.'

And as if ashamed, she hid her face beneath her headscarf.

Just then her husband arrived back from work, young, stout and robust as ever, and called out to her from the yard.

'Coming,' she replied, gaily skipping down Thomas's crumbling steps.

'We'll talk again,' she said to Thomas, who had followed her out, troubled and dejected.

Yannis was standing on his own doorstep and Maria said to him laughing, 'Yannis, Yannis, guess what nearly happened today... You were very nearly cuckolded by Thomas... it was touch and go... He's a regular wild boar!'*

Her husband looked startled for a moment and with his innocent half-closed eyes gazed first at Thomas, who lowered his head and started trembling, and then directly at his wife.

Maria, still laughing, stared contemptuously at the old man. Then Yannis himself started laughing heartily and signalled to Maria to follow him inside.

Thomas shook his head slyly and muttered, as if talking to himself but loud enough for others to hear, 'By St Spyridon, Argyris gave me sound advice today... We're all agreed... and I'll do everything he asks me. I'll consult the notary next time I see him. That should please Maria too... and...'

# VI

It was another afternoon towards the end of summer. The sun was about to set, gilding all the mountain peaks. Inside Argyris's house, Chrysanthi was alone in the living-room just then, slowly tidying up and muttering to herself, her aged bony head wobbling a little.

'Worry is consuming my poor Argyris,' she murmured, 'and he's such a good soul, such a good family man! His mind is always dwelling on the welfare of the family and every day they try his patience; day or night he never gets a moment's peace. Give us this! Take care of that! Help us here! Don't meddle there! — when the sea stops surging, his poor head will get a rest. As a result his asthma keeps returning, it gets worse by the day... And yet he looks as strong as any ox! Tall and stout and handsome as you please. But he only has to get a bit annoyed, walk up the slightest hill, or find some business deal is not straightforward and he becomes pale as death, gets out of breath and starts panting like a dog in summer. What a life, poor man! Whereas that baggage... She eats, drinks, beds her husband, shouts and raises merry hell without turning a hair. Tough as nails! Yannis is strong too and he's for ever laughing, laughing like a halfwit. And she's so stuck up... She goes to church and the women all turn round and gape at her; they're so jealous she often gets the evil eye;* and she wears so much jewellery to dances she lights up the whole square, confound her! As if we don't have baubles too! I've just as much jewellery as she, I wear it just as often and we're always present on the same occasions! But alas, I've now grown old. Life's almost over. How is one to undo the ravages of time? My hair's turned white, my teeth are falling out, my head now wobbles and I'm full of wrinkles; happy days, alas, are over! Yet she seems to grow younger... Her cheeks are rosy and when she gets angry they positively glow. She works, perspires and looks about for more, but never once falls ill. Ah me!'

And as she rambled on like this, she bent and swept the rubbish out through the door with a short brush of myrtle twigs.

A little later the priest's wife arrived, spinning as she walked. Chrysanthi greeted her smilingly and said, 'And how are things with you today?'

'Very well, thank you, sister-in-law,' she replied, twirling her spindle as she halted in front of her.

'Come and sit inside . . . It's cooler there, with the breezes from the window.'

The two women went indoors. The priest's wife detached her distaff from her belt, put it in the corner by the window and came and sat on the big chest.

'I brought my distaff to avoid going through the square with my arms dangling,' she said. 'It's cumbersome, but the men are always on the lookout for an excuse to gossip; they sit there slandering any woman who goes past . . . By the way, where's Maria?'

'She'll be back any minute,' replied Chrysanthi, her head wobbling as she sat down beside the table. 'She had something to see to in the field and asked if you could wait for her. Would you like some coffee?'

'Oh, don't bother! . . . Where are you off to now?'

'Me? Nowhere. My daughter's in the kitchen. She's just back from the wash and is sorting out the laundry. She's already lit a fire, so it really is no trouble.'

She called out, 'Aglaïa, make the priest's wife a coffee, would you, and one for me as well . . .'

'My husband will be round here shortly with my father,' said the priest's wife.

'No doubt about that little business, eh? Well, they're very welcome.'

'Yes, *our* business . . .' said the priest's wife slightly nettled, feeling that Chrysanthi should not be so interested in the affairs of others.

'Ah good,' said Chrysanthi. 'My husband says it's always best to settle matters swiftly; have they found a solution yet?'

Just then Aglaïa, a plump girl of fifteen in bare feet and with her sleeves rolled up came in; after greeting the priest's wife, she took two cups down from the shelf and promptly left the room.

'Argyris is an outsider,' said the priest's wife, 'and his opinion doesn't count. Everything is up to Yannis. He is my sister's husband and he'll tell her what to do — whether she should agree or not!'

'You know very well,' replied Chrysanthi irritably, 'that my Argyris, long may he live, is the helmsman of this household.* Yannis won't move so much as this without consulting him.' And she indicated the tip of her little finger. 'Quite right too: the whole village says Argyris has more brains; he even gives advice to strangers; people come round here to consult him as if he were a lawyer! He asks Yannis his opinion as a mere formality... because my Argyris is a formal person. And as you know, the brothers are as devoted as two angels, however much we wives may quarrel. That's only natural: when they were little their half-brothers persecuted them, so Yannis heeding his mother latched onto Argyris, who raised him, married him off and provided his bride with as much jewellery as me... When their father died while Yannis was still small, my Argyris took him and their mother in and the three of them set up house together; so now Yannis still regards him as his father.'

Just then, Aglaïa came in with a cup of coffee in each hand, and after serving the two women, left the room without a word; the priest's wife followed her with her eyes.

'A good girl,' she observed, 'quiet and discreet.'

'Yes,' said Chrysanthi proudly, 'we're teaching our daughters to be well behaved. My husband is very sensible and doesn't want them giving themselves airs. He wants them to do their chores from first to last and not get bored or be ashamed of work. Just so long as they don't become domestic servants! We draw the line at that. He wants this so they can marry someone ordinary if they wish. Genteel people expect fat dowries and they're not always the best bet. Often it's the more vulgar sort who prosper most. And if we wait for somebody genteel, they may end up on the shelf like all their maiden aunts. And as you know, my dear, we are all in total agreement with my husband. Naturally, he's our helmsman after all...'

'Our helmsman...' smiled the priest's wife ironically.

'Yes, our helmsman,' affirmed the other. 'We agree with him about this and every other matter, because whatever he proposes is for the common good, and we're a devoted family, as God decrees... So what, if we sometimes...'

'Devoted!' exclaimed the other woman. 'But Chrysanthi, you hardly speak to my sister, and when you do you're immediately at daggers drawn! You're most peculiar, both of you... The only time you call a truce is for half an hour before you take communion, and the very same day you start quarrelling again!'

'Never mind all that... Our little tiffs do not divide us. Which family doesn't have its quarrels? We've got along this way for years... but as regards the common good, we're always in agreement. Look at brothers, when they're little they fight and squabble all day long... my

Argiris used to beat his brother soundly, almost every day! But when they grew up all was forgotten and now they get on like a house on fire. It's the same with us, for goodness sake! . . . and our husbands never hear us.'

By now they had both finished their coffee; the priest's wife placed her cup upside down on the saucer and put it on the table; Chrysanthi got up and put it and her own cup on the shelf. Then she went across to the window and looked down the road.

The two women continued their interminable conversation.

After a while Chrysanthi remarked, 'Maria's back.'

'So she is,' said the priest's wife, leaning out of the adjacent window.

Spread out to left and right below them was the rambling village, with its imposing yellow church in the middle and its blackened uneven tiled roofs, smoke rising from many of them at that time of day. Near the centre of the village the houses were all built very close together, along ridges, down gullies and on level ground, some small, others large, all with tiny windows, some ancient others new, some rendered, others in plain stone, some set unevenly along crooked alleys, others fronting the main street or meeting it end-on; but towards the outskirts they stood further apart in their own gardens, extending up a gentle hill with clusters of bamboo, then down towards the outer limits of the village, where olive trees displayed their bushy, silvery-green foliage in the ravines.

The main street divided the village from one end to the other down the middle, but from Argyris's window it looked more like a sort of chasm between the blackened roofs, and only emerged into the open at the edge of the main village, where it turned a corner and descended, broad and white, to the foot of the next hill dotted with houses and bamboo clumps, then continued straight for a short distance only to disappear behind a hillock covered with silvery-green olive trees and dusky cypresses and crowned with a pretty yellow church with its modest belfry and three little bells.

Making their way along this road just then were about two hundred sheep, clustered together in a single flock, their little feet pattering swiftly and rhythmically, their timid heads nodding close to the ground; and here and there among them were a few goats, pressing forward with their heads held high, glancing to left and right, ready to break into a run. Behind the flock was a stretch of empty road choked with rising dust, and after that came a motley crowd of women of all ages — old crones, matrons and unmarried women, even young lasses minding little children, some with round baskets on their heads, others with bundles of split wood or twigs, some with infants in their arms, others spinning with their distaffs or goading on their laden beasts — and as they moved down the road in little groups, all of them were chatting away, making noise enough for the sound to reach the village. Behind them was another stretch of empty road. Then came a man with a plough over his shoulder leading a black ox roped by its horns; and just rounding the bend beneath the hill with the olive trees and little church came Thomas's donkey, a bundle of sticks tied to one side of its saddle and Maria on its back, followed by Thomas himself, clean-shaven, in new *tsarouchia* and straw hat,* goading the beast with his thick stick.

They could not be made out distinctly from the window, but Chrysanthi had spotted them at once.

The flock slowly drew closer to the village, leaving a cloud of dust in its wake. By now the first sheep could be heard and their bleating steadily grew louder. At last the flock reached the beginning of the main village and below the first hill with houses, at the foot of the steep slope leading to that neighbourhood, one group of sheep halted and held back, separating from the main flock before surging at the double up the slope. Several women followed, scrambling up behind them. The rest of the sheep continued on their way. And as the flock passed by the houses in the village it kept diminishing, as many sheep remained behind, either halting before their homes or disappearing along alleys, so that less than half the flock reached the foot of the hill leading up to Argyris's house.

The sheep were the first to reach the house, bleating and coming to a halt under the trellis. Aglaïa rushed to open up the stable doors and the sheep disappeared inside. Soon Maria's two daughters also returned bearing provisions on their heads, Amalia with a pannier of split logs, Olga with a bundle of twigs, their hatchets tucked into their belts. Andreas, blond, lanky, round-shouldered and ungainly as ever, arrived back with them and smiling toothily gave them a hand down with their loads, while also taking the opportunity to give Amalia's breast a tweak.

At last Maria too reached the shade of the trellis, with Thomas just behind her. They halted the donkey, which wanted to continue on to Thomas's shed, hissing at it through their lips, and Maria jumped lithely from its back and shook out her skirts. Holding the beast by its halter, Thomas watched her anxiously with sparkling eyes, stroking his white moustache and even glancing down at himself with a sad wry smile.

Laughing and looking at him mockingly she said, 'Good on you, Thomas... thanks for the ride.'

Thomas gave her a radiant smile of pleasure.

'Well, let's unload the donkey,' he then said to Andreas.

Maria turned her back on them and disappeared round the corner of the house, while together the old man and the lad started unfastening the ropes.

'Free the end hanging from the saddle-bow!' Andreas told him.

Thomas flushed red and glared at him, on the point of flaring up, but then controlled himself, realizing that the lad had meant no harm.

'Hanging from the saddle-bow, eh!' he growled.

'Oh, Thomas, I didn't mean anything,' the boy protested in alarm, 'I just meant the rope... Don't have me whipped tonight.'

'Just watch your mouth then,' he replied, his arm raised threateningly, but calming down and smiling.

By this time Maria was already upstairs and before even entering the living-room she burst into uproarious laughter. Tugging at her rosy cheeks and without waiting to see who was in the room, she exclaimed, 'Goodness, that Hangman Thomas... there's no restraining him... The way he carries on... like a wild boar!... Ha, ha, ha!'

Then noticing the priest's wife she bade her good evening and, still convulsed with laughter, gave Chrysanthi a look.

'What's all this about, what have you been up to!' the priest's wife scolded her, unconsciously adopting her husband's lofty manner. 'You must be going mad, Maria!'

And she shook her head several times, pursing her lips.

'Like a wild boar!' Maria repeated and again laughed heartily.

Chrysanthi gave the priest's wife a knowing smile.

'My nephews and nieces will soon be Thomas's heirs!' she said maliciously.

Maria turned on her and replied aggressively, 'People's mugs are a mirror of their hearts! Pale-faced people are never pure, it's malice that turns them pale and makes their heads wobble... As for poor me, I am merely following the advice of wise Argyris... Particularly if I say no!'

Chrysanthi did not reply and all three of them remained silent for a few moments.

Finally Yannis's voice was heard in the yard admonishing his children and trying without success to appear firm: 'Tonight you're to stay quietly with Aglaïa; we have things to discuss upstairs, so don't keep running in and out... Otherwise your mother will give you a good spanking... So just watch out...'

And he laughed. The two boys laughed with him, clinging to his hands and clothes and trying to hinder him as he came up the stairs, a happy smile beneath his drooping moustache, his sleepy eyes half-closed.

'Now you stay outside,' he told them, fending them off gently with his hands.

As soon as she noticed him, Maria laughingly cried out, 'As God is my witness, Yannis, Thomas is out to cuckold you! You'd better take precautions... There's no restraining him... You wouldn't believe how he's been behaving! Goodness me, like a wild boar!'

'Ha, ha, ha!' laughed Yannis, coming in without the children and bidding everyone good-evening.

# VII

They had all assembled in the living-room, except for Chrysanthi who had withdrawn discreetly to the kitchen, as it was none of her business.

The two sisters — the priest's wife and Maria — were seated on the large carved chest, one on the end with her feet resting on the floor, the other in the middle, dangling her legs and swinging them whenever she wished to speak.

Yannis was sitting on a little bench at his wife's feet, his sleeves rolled up, his hairy chest exposed, his sleepy eyes half closed; he had taken off his hat and was playing with it and occasionally fanning his fat face.

Sitting hunched on a stool beside him, his stout stick held in both hands between his knees, was the emaciated notary, looking even older this evening, with his translucent skin, his hectic cheeks and the smile that never vanished even when he was annoyed.

Argyris, having difficulty breathing, was leaning back in his chair, his shoulders resting against the table with its red, white and blue striped woollen cloth in the middle of the room, and every now and then his lively little eyes would blink and dart about.

And finally, seated grandly opposite the notary was his son-in-law the handsome priest, a tall man with noble features and large fine eyes under his greying brow, wearing a clean black cassock fastened with a scarlet sash, and a soft hat. With his feet together under his greenish surplice, his right hand resting on the arm of his chair and his head held high, he looked as if he were addressing his congregation from the rostrum of his church.

'Come to an agreement,' the notary was saying in his scarcely audible voice, which issued like a dying breath from between his rosy lips. 'Come to an agreement like brothers and sisters, like the family we are. I don't want to retain anything for myself, I know my old age is quite secure. How much longer do I have to live? Two or three more years? Maybe, maybe not! The Reverend here is a man of God, how could he let me die in the gutter? He'll give me the same food he eats himself and if I'm dissatisfied under his roof, I can always come here to my dear Maria for a crust of bread. How could she refuse me? The

Lord be praised, she has enough to feed ten men like me ...'

Then Argyris, closing his little eyes, observed, 'It is also a matter of plain justice! In the codicils to date, the Reverend has been given all the land.'

The priest's wife gave him a sidelong glance and said impatiently, 'Yannis, you've heard what father has to say. Now let's hear from you; the house is the only thing we disagree about! But I want us to discuss it all with you; Yannis, are you listening?'

Yannis laughed and made no reply.

'Upon my oath,' said the priest, deepening his voice grandly as he did in church when reading from the Gospel, 'the house as it stands is undoubtedly worth something, but what if it were divided into three — because of course our father will retain part of it to serve him as his chambers, he can't conduct his business in the street, for heaven's sake, now can he?'

'Of course, of course!' said Yannis hastily, feeling obligated to say something, without having quite followed the priest's elaborate syntax.

'What d'you mean, of course?' said Maria, tossing her head angrily. 'We have ...'

'The house,' the priest's wife interrupted her, 'is in a completely different neighbourhood; what would you do with it? If it were close by here, I could understand.'

'Of course,' Yannis at once repeated with a smile, feeling he should make some reply himself.

Maria turned towards him angrily and nudged him with her foot.

'We have two male children,' she said, 'and time is not standing still; soon one of them will be getting married and we'll need to put him in the house down there; otherwise we'll go mad in here for lack of space ... How are we all supposed to fit in here, hugger-mugger like the gypsies ...'*

'Of course, of course,' Yannis agreed immediately with a complacent chuckle.

'Oh, God will provide before then!' said the priest grandly 'Who can presume to know His ways?' — and he crossed himself. 'I myself have no patrimonial home; I let my brother have it, since I'd found a higher calling ... I let him have it just like that, for my sins, I gifted it to him! I didn't demand land in compensation, only a few trinkets we agreed on over coffee, so I too could say I had inherited something from my father. And that's the truth, so help me God! . . .'

Argyris was looking nervously around the room.

'The house,' said the notary in his faint voice, 'is best left undivided just the way it is; let the priest's wife and her children have it and I'll stay on with them. Fate restored it to single ownership with me, and I don't want to see it split up again in my lifetime. I understand the ownership must change, but to have it divided into four again? . . .'

And sighing and smiling his involuntary smile, he continued, 'God did not see fit to spare my only son, your brother . . . He's been dead for years now, but I've not forgotten him, his death was a real blow. He'd be a man by now, a father, even a grandfather perhaps . . . He would have inherited the whole house, but now I shall take my sorrow to the grave. We were three brothers and my father made us all notaries like himself. He managed to provide us with a little education: he had the means in those days, thanks to the British and the old nobility.* Then our elder brother, Markos, may he bless us from on high, became a priest and set up on his own, and we let him have our mother's house; that left two — counting my father, three — notaries under the same roof. Shortly afterwards our mother died, and then my brother's only son died too — a tall strapping lad he was! . . . It seems he drank cold water after sweating, caught a chill and within six months was under ground! My sister-in-law had no more children after that. Then came my brother's turn, he too was taken from us; and when our father, aged a hundred, closed his eyes, I inherited the whole house and the land. I had one son and you two girls but then the village was visited by a smallpox epidemic; it cut down about seventy children, all the young ones . . . my son, alas, among them . . . So then I closed my books, left you two with your mother and went abroad to forget my sorrow, finally returning ten years later just in time to close your mother's eyes and marry you two off. Ah! I've seen so many deaths! My eyes have seen so much! While abroad, I met with great misfortune . . .'

'Let's get back to our discussion,' said Argyris, seeing that time was getting on and knowing that once the notary started relating all his bygone woes they would be there all night, 'and let's admit that . . .'

'Let's hear from you, Yannis,' the priest's wife interrupted, turning to him.

'My wife's bridesmaid . . .' said the notary in his faint voice.

'Your wife's bridesmaid . . .' protested the priest gravely, 'how can you mention her in my presence? I'm a man of the cloth and a spiritual leader ... I have a position to maintain.'

'Old age addles the mind,' said his wife, by way of excusing her father. 'You must forgive him, dear.'

'My wife's bridesmaid,' continued the notary, 'advises me not to divide the land and says I mustn't be unfair to either of you; she's equally fond of both of you, you see ...'

'That woman,' said Maria laughing bitterly, 'has been the ruin of you from the start. She wants to bleed you dry. She never left you a penny in your pocket. Today you'd be a man of standing and we'd be rich, as you were doing quite well with all your legal work.'

'Enough, let's change the subject,' said the priest, raising his large hand.

'That woman,' said the notary, his lifeless voice trembling a little, 'has been slandered more than anyone because of me, she is hated by you and the community and treated with contempt for my sake. She sold her land for me when I ran into trouble, she's put up with me for fifteen years now and grown old in my arms, yet she's never asked me for a thing, not even to get married. I'd have her if she wanted because she's always helped me out. And whenever I listened to her I prospered. And when I didn't, her words came back to haunt me. But I deliberately ignore her, so she doesn't take it for granted and start saying she's the boss ...'

'In that case,' declared the priest in exasperation, 'go and discuss things with your wife's bridesmaid, our meeting here is pointless.'

'He's right!' Maria said emphatically.

'Ah!' sighed the priest's wife, 'he's lost all sense of shame in his old age.'

'But where's the harm?' laughed Yannis good-naturedly. 'Our poor old father-in-law just wants a bit of crumpet in old age. So what, if he's old? Good on him! Ha, ha, ha!' And as he said this, he played with his straw hat.

No one laughed and the women looked at the priest nervously.

Argyris, closing his little eyes, said to Yannis, 'Well, are you going to discuss your little business or aren't you? It's getting dark already! Light the lamp, someone.'

Maria went and took a bronze four-wicked lamp down from the shelf, placed it on the table, filled it with oil and trimmed it, then asked her husband for a match and lit two wicks. Slowly the light pervaded the room, though the windows were still bright, and everybody looked at one another.

The notary, responding to Argyris, said, 'We can always settle things some other time.'

'He's remembered his wife's bridesmaid and has changed his mind,' exclaimed Maria. 'He needs to consult her first.'

Argyris looked at the priest and shrugged; the notary started to get up.

'Sit down, father,' the priest's wife urged him. 'Perhaps we can still reach an agreement.'

'Let's assume,' said Maria, 'that we let you have the house, will you then compensate us?'

'Of course,' replied the priest's wife promptly.

Here the priest finally lost patience.

'Of course, what d'you mean of course?' he said. 'Surely we're not going to follow the old-timers, we're not going to use their system for calculating compensation! The house, they'd say, has so many beams, each worth so much, totalling so much; so many floorboards, totalling so much; so many roof-tiles, at so much per thousand, totalling so much; so many square metres of wall, so many doors, so many windows, totalling so much . . . I could go on and on!'

And as he rattled off each item, he struck the palm of one hand with two fingers of the other.

'How do we do it then?' asked Yannis, feeling he ought to say something too.

'Not like that!' snapped the priest. 'We'll just say: the house is now old and worth roughly so much.'

Then suddenly Argyris came up with a proposal: 'In exchange for half the house, Reverend, you'll give my sister-in-law your property at Fano, including the hut, the field and the fifteen sapling olive trees! . . .'

'Yes, the property at Fano!' Yannis hastily agreed and laughed.

The priest became very agitated.

'But that's part of my estate, what's it got to do with my wife's dowry!'

Then after a moment's reflection he continued, 'Oh well, we're not getting anywhere, so let's leave the house undivided and father can dispose of it in his will as he sees fit! Or just let things stay the way they are.'

He rose, taking up the full height of the low room.

'No...' said the notary, suddenly changing his mind. 'My wife's bridesmaid will get the idea that I'm following her advice. Let's settle things now... Anyway, it's not fair for the priest's wife to have everything and Maria to be excluded from her mother's dowry! My assets were a separate matter: each daughter received her dowry, the rest was mine to do with as I pleased!'

The priest sat down again.

'But how come,' said the priest's wife, 'Yannis and my sister haven't said a word, how come we've only heard from you, Argyris? No offence, but would you like it if I started interfering over Chrysanthi's dowry?'

'Yannis is irresolute,' replied Argyris, 'and goes along with everything, it's always "up to you, Sir!"'

Yannis laughed.

'I don't wish to be considered greedy...' said the priest, swinging one leg, 'since I am a minister of the Almighty... But let's assume that in return for half the house I were to provide compensation from my estate, not of course Fano but some other property, if that were acceptable... Well then, let's discuss which other properties...'

'You could surrender your wife's dowry,' observed Argyris eagerly.

'Surrender it,' echoed Yannis, amused by the serious tone of the discussion.

'No...' replied the priest obstinately.

'My house doesn't amount to much without her dowry,' said the notary.

They continued wrangling for hours, raising their voices, losing their tempers, all talking at once, but at long last they reached an agreement. In exchange for the celebrated half house, Maria would receive the priest's property at Fano, including the hut and the field, but not the fifteen olive trees.

Then Argyris smiled and said, 'Well that's settled, from tomorrow each will assume ownership of his own property. Now bring us some wine, Maria, so the priest can give his blessing to our agreement, and call Chrysanthi in as well.'

'We're not on speaking terms,' replied Maria scowling.

Just then Thomas appeared at the door, peering into the house as if he wished to speak to someone. Argyris invited him to join them for a drink, so he stepped inside and greeted the assembly.

'The notary,' Argyris told him, 'has just divided his property between his daughters. He too is getting on and finds he cannot manage any longer. Come and drink his health...'

Thomas gave a cunning smile.

'Has he really made everything over to his daughters?' he asked.

'Yes,' Argyris replied uneasily.

'To his daughters,' he repeated, shaking his head and looking Maria in the eye, 'his entire estate? So now he can no longer sell off anything himself... Though he couldn't before of course, as his sons-in-law wouldn't have allowed it... And how could an outsider get involved in such a tangled business... And the house?...'

'That too,' said Maria, laughing as he kept on looking at her.

'But why to his daughters?' persisted Thomas. 'Couldn't he have found an outsider? And if his daughters get fed up with him tomorrow, what's an elderly man like him to do? Better an outsider than one's own kith and kin, wasn't that what you said to me, Argyris? He may live to regret it!'

'You're jumping to conclusions, Thomas,' the priest told him condescendingly.

'You're quite right, Thomas,' said Argyris sweetly, 'but horses for courses... His daughters are his own flesh and blood, whereas you are childless...'

'A man who has no offspring of his own,' said Thomas bitterly, 'is like a solitary bird on the bough! Such is my lot. I know what I should and shouldn't do. I know what I might live to regret... However reason doesn't always decide things... and man doesn't always follow his own best interests, but on the contrary does what he knows will bring him harm. I came over, Argyris, to ask you to arrange the life annuity that we discussed. The notary's here and could advise us...'

'What's this,' exclaimed Maria, getting angry, 'is Argyris taking over your property?'

'We both are,' Yannis reassured her smiling. 'We're brothers, aren't we? Why should it be me and not Argyris, why Argyris and not me?'

'A splendid idea,' said the priest grandly. 'Why would an elderly person like yourself, who can no longer work, want to chase around doing chores and looking after property... This way, you'll have a fixed income, come rain or shine, and can take things easy.' Maria glared at Thomas and Argyris angrily, and Thomas realized that she was none too pleased.

'Should I make it over to you personally?' he asked her plaintively.

'A woman,' said the notary in his faint voice, lowering his eyes as if embarrassed, 'can't do the slightest thing against her husband's wishes... She can't so much as move... What guarantees would you have with an undertaking from a married woman?'*

'And I,' said Yannis, 'can't do anything without my brother. How would I pay up? He's the helmsman of our family.'

The priest gave him an approving look.

'Even so,' observed Argyris, closing his eyes, 'five drachmas a day, no... no... I don't think we can run to that... After all, you'll be getting your food, a share of what I eat myself, and then your housekeeping, your clothing and... whatever else your heart desires... What more d'you want? Isn't all that worth at least a fiver? Alright, let's say we throw in some pocket money, a drachma a day to spend as you see fit... What more d'you want? In round figures seventy fivers a year... What d'you say? Sound reasonable? You'd still have the right to demand the fiver, but only if we neglect your needs; I say this only because we walk through life hand in hand with death. I might die and my heirs fail to satisfy you. I'm being honest and upfront with you. Well, what d' you say?'

'Yes, that's right...' said the priest craftily, getting up from his chair.

'Whatever you say,' said Thomas cunningly, looking at Maria.

She smiled back at him.

# VIII

The life annuity had been signed a few days later and time had moved on. Then one day Argyris decided to demolish Thomas's house and rebuild it with an upper storey, incorporating it into his own. He had ordered two tons of stone, which had been unloaded on the beach, selected marble from the mountain quarry for the doors and windows, arranged for several cypress trees to be cut down, hiring carpenters to shape them into beams and planks, and taken delivery of cement and sand, which the women in the family transported on their heads, while Thomas with his donkey carted the stone up from the beach, making five trips a day in his eagerness to please Maria. Heaps of stone accumulated round his house, piling higher in his yard and little garden by the day, and every evening the fresh cypress planks would be delivered, filling the air with their fragrance, and stacked next to Argyris's storeroom. When the villagers ran across Argyris in the street, they would smilingly congratulate him while privately spitting on him with contempt, and the entire village condemned Thomas with one voice, cursing him for having behaved unjustly to his nephews in favour of outsiders.

The summer months were over but the weather had not yet broken. It was a beautiful sunny October day and noon was approaching. Just then Thomas was coming up the hill from the beach towards the village, prodding his donkey from behind as he entered a stretch of road which led through an olive grove planted on a verdant slope. The majestic olive trees, with their branching boughs and silvery-green foliage, were weighed down by their bounteous crop, which glistened like gold among the tiny leaves. The grove was like a park, with no thorny bushes, weeds or heather growing wild under the trees, because the owners had cleared the ground ready for the rich crop to fall, so it was covered only by lush verdant grass. The road was an ancient one dating back to Hellenic times, paved with broad white stones, and wound its way like a serpent between the massive olive trees. It had not been repaired for centuries yet was still substantially intact, though in some places stones were missing and in others it was half buried under soil washed down from the steep banks and now overgrown. Further along it entered a little ravine between two high ridges, the precipitous sides of which revealed the rugged strata of the underlying rock, yellowish, bereft of vegetation and eroded by the sun and rain.

Thomas's patient little beast was struggling up the steep slope, two large stones tied to its saddle, and every so often it would pause to regain its footing, or to gather momentum before tackling a step in the uneven road, or to choose the easiest way forward, while Thomas himself trudged along behind, bent, flushed and sweating, his jacket over one shoulder, prodding the animal with his stick, helping it when it faltered by pushing at the saddle-bow or heaving on the saddle with both arms, repeatedly shouting 'Giddy-up! Giddy-up!' and even conversing with it now and then: 'Keep going, you stupid ass, keep going until you too drop, you poor old thing! Despite it all, your life is easier than mine! . . . Giddy-up! Giddy-up!' And he would whack it with his stick. 'Giddy-up! . . . You've still got many a stone to carry. You're not losing heart already, are you? . . . Giddy-up! . . . It's going to be a regular seraglio, my house . . . their house! It'll be built onto theirs and have two more windows, making an extra room even larger than their living-room! And of course Maria will get it with her share when they divide things! . . . So that's where she'll be sleeping with her husband! . . . Ah! Ah! She's not aged a bit, her cheeks are blooming, what a woman! She devours a fellow with her eyes! . . . Giddy-up! . . . But no favours so far: how much longer is she going to keep me waiting? She's evading me by playing the coquette! Now they've taken everything I own . . . Nothing left at all . . . And their children, curse them, are forever at me . . . even in the house, and no one ticks them off. Why, oh why, must they all do this? She enjoys laughing at me and makes fun of me! . . . Is that what I gave my property away for? . . . She seems to think so! . . . Well, I can get nasty too . . . Nothing gained by being nice! . . . I'll just grab her and to hell with consequences! . . . Even God sometimes uses force.'

By now he was entering the little ravine and the donkey quickened its pace, as the road just there was straighter and unpaved beneath its sandy surface. Thomas was smiling, as if entranced by some delightful daydream, and in a high-pitched voice he began to sing his customary song:

>  *Beautiful a beauty is, five or ten times over,*
>  *But best of all's a woman with her lover.*

Suddenly from the top of the ridge a child's silvery voice piped up:

'Hangman Tho-o-o-mas!'

The old man started back at once, halted his donkey and, dropping his jacket to the ground, stared about with bloodshot eyes, his face flushing as he began to lose control. Unable to see anyone high or low, he half-jestingly replied, 'Here I am, my boy, here I am . . . What is it that your mother wants?'

Then picking up his jacket he beat the donkey angrily, cursing it and shouting, 'Giddy-up! . . . Could even the trees be now acquiring speech?'

From the opposite ridge another child's voice again called out, 'Hangman Tho-o-o-mas!'

Now the old man completely lost his temper.

'My children . . . my children,' he shouted out again, 'what is it you want, my children?'

Again he took his spleen out on the donkey, cursing it and giving it another vicious whack. 'Giddy-up! Devil take you . . . Giddy-up!'

Laughter rang out from both sides of the ravine and Thomas realized that many children had gathered up there, waiting for him to come by.

'Oh God!' he sighed.

And now a third voice cried out: 'Hangman Tho-o-o-mas, I can see you, I can see you!'

'You're right,' he said laughing and grinding his few teeth. 'You're absolutely right, it's all my stupid fault for having fathered you, yes me, my little bastards.'

'Hangman Tho-o-o-mas,' cried two or three voices at once, after the gales of laughter had subsided.

'Giddy-up . . . Goddamn your hide,' he cried, beating the donkey. 'Giddy-up! Just a little further along here in the ditch, yes down here, this is where I used to pleasure all your mothers! This is where I sowed you all. If only I had had more sense . . . Now you've every right to call me names. Serves me damn well right!'

Again he heard the laughter of the children, who were following him high along the ridge-top. In desperation he hurried on out of the ravine, hoping that once he reached the open road he would find someone to protect him; and all the while he kept looking up, trying to recognize some child's face among the leaves, so that later when he came across him he could thrash him.

One of them piped up again, 'I see you, but you can't see me!'

Others chimed in amid hilarious laughter: 'Hangman Tho-o-o-mas! I see you, I see you!'

He continued to respond in the same manner, pretending to be relishing the joke.

At last he came out onto the open road and the children's taunting ended. But for a while he could still hear their receding laughter as they ran off through the woods. Sighing from the bottom of his heart, he muttered, 'What a nightmare!' and tears welled up in his eyes. 'It's always me, always me they find to pick on, no one else in the whole village! But why, why? . . .' And he gave his donkey yet another whack.

Just then he caught sight of his sister Anastasia up ahead; his first impulse was to take another path, as he suddenly felt ashamed; he was afraid she would upbraid him for turning her out on the day of his wife's funeral and for having secretly arranged a life annuity with strangers. He had not set eyes on her since the day he had been widowed. Now it seemed to him that the old woman had aged even more: in the daylight her pale face looked drier, more wizened and more ugly, with those faded restless eyes, red with weeping.

'Oh, Thomas!' she said, 'Thomas! . . .'

He stopped and stared at her stupidly, as the patient donkey continued on its way.

'Anastasia!' he exclaimed, not knowing what else to say.

'You've dug your own grave!' she said, 'and it hurts me to see it because you're my brother and we're born of the same mother. I came down here deliberately to find you and talk things over . . . But it's a bit late now . . . What have you done, Thomas . . . What possessed you?'

He glared at her.

'Something's been bothering you . . .' he said. 'Ah, I know, I know! . . . You wanted everything for your own children, the poor things . . . that's it!'

'I didn't want you to be treated with contempt,' she said and her eyes filled with tears.

He looked her in the eyes again and suddenly realised that no one else in the whole world would ever gaze at him with such concern, no one else would shed a tear for him.

'Well, it's done now!' he told her hoarsely with a sigh. 'But why should I be the village laughing-stock? Every evening at home the girls going to the well call out my nickname; now they even do so on the street, the old mules! I have no life. Why? But why?'

'Because you're alone and unprotected!'

'Ever since my wife died!'

'You heeded the advice of that bloodsucker Argyris... and threw us out!'

'Ever since, I've been wretched and alone!' he said shaking his head bitterly.

'Ever since!... And now that you've made over your property to them, you've lost everyone's respect. People know why you did it... That whore has led you up the garden path and now she's laughing at you...'

'That whore!' said Thomas, his hackles rising. 'Who? Who!'

'Calm down,...' she told him, 'don't get angry with me... I only want what's best for you, even though you threw us out; I'm the only person in the world who cares for you; she is simply making fun of you, while cursing and abusing you behind your back... Oh, Thomas!'

He made no reply but quickened his pace to catch up with the donkey, which by now was some distance ahead, knowing its own way home. His sister followed at his heels.

'Things will only go from bad to worse with this obsession of yours, poor fellow...' she went on. 'Is this how an elderly man should carry on? You've lost your self-respect and reputation. Is it worth it, only to become the village laughing-stock?'

He gave her another despairing look.

'Ah, life can't go on like this much longer,' he said. 'If I can't see a way out, I'll end it once and for all, like this!'

And he pinched his gullet between finger and thumb, making a choking sound and rolling back his eyes.

'Argyris is driving you to this to inherit everything without incurring costs...' she said.

They walked on in silence for some distance. She resumed her spinning, using her spit to moisten the weft as it emerged thick and pliant from the ball of wool and was twisted and strengthened by the turning spindle, dangling from the distaff almost to the ground, while he pushed the donkey from behind to make it go faster up the road. Finally the old woman continued: 'You'd do well to remain silent when they taunt you, you know, because people are spiteful and the more you answer back the more they'll laugh at you. Besides, you yourself say such peculiar things, and in such a weird way, that people can't help laughing and you make yourself ridiculous. Don't you see? If you want to do something about it, grab a child and smash its head or break its leg and go to jail, then when you come out you'll see how people fear you... But carrying on like this? You're not the only person in the village, for God's sake, everybody, man or woman, has a nickname to identify them, yet nobody behaves like you. What's wrong with you!'

And she crossed herself.

He looked at her again despondently and shook his head.

Then Anastasia began telling him about her children. One of her sons was about to join the army and her elder daughter's dowry was now complete, even though her uncle had not given her a thing from all her aunt had left behind, not a blessed thing... All her belongings would doubtless have been taken by Argyris's family, by Chrysanthi, the old prune, and by Maria, Mistress Maria... for their precious Amalia and their precious Aglaïa! Of course they would, of course!... Mind you, Amalia was turning into a real peach, prettier even than her mother. Pinching and romping with her cousin all day long, not a day went by without someone spotting them together, so she'd better watch out too! Whereas Anastasia's own daughter was a good girl, honest innocent and virtuous like all her children. One more virtuous than the other! They all respected her and were hard workers, first rate workers! And the land yielded them their daily bread, little though it was, and they even worked as hired hands and so never needed to borrow so much as a fiver! And now she was marrying her daughter off to a good man who had requested her; the wedding was to take place at Shrovetide and Thomas would of course be welcome to come and join in the festivities; they would be slaughtering a lamb, the lamb their ewe was expecting in November...

Meanwhile they were approaching the fork in the road leading up the hill to Thomas's house. The donkey took a few rapid steps, gathering momentum to climb the steep path, and the old woman bade her brother farewell.

'As I said,' she reminded him, still spinning, 'don't answer back in that peculiar way. Don't forget now!'

'When I get angry,' he replied, 'I say the first thing that comes into my head, I can't help myself. My mind starts conceiving all these weird notions and I just have to spit them out! What gets into me the Devil only knows.'

He began to climb the hill after the donkey; half way up he turned and looked back at the bent figure of his sister making her way home, mumbling to herself as she went.

'Who knows whether I'd have been better off with them,' he said to himself, 'if I hadn't turned them out that time... My nephews and nieces would have been more compassionate than strangers and would have defended me... But how was I to know that Anastasia really cared about me? I had no idea... I assumed the worst because I myself am evil.' He sighed. 'And then there is Maria!...'

# IX

Thomas halted underneath the vine, which was now beginning to turn yellow and shed its leaves. He looked about and then called out, 'Maria...'

'I've another devil on my back just now,' she shouted angrily from upstairs, 'must you come pestering me too? Unload as best you can. The pitchfork is down there.'

And she went on cursing her sister-in-law in muted tones: 'He heard us... of course he did... What are you trying to do to me, you mummy?'

The old man sighed, then bracing one side of the saddle with the wooden pitchfork, he loosened the rope round the large stone on the other and suddenly released it, letting it fall to the ground with a thud.

Meanwhile Chrysanthi was answering Maria back: 'Thomas's property doesn't all belong to you, you know, we own half of it. You secured it with your body, you miserable slut, even the old man didn't disgust you, you're so greedy! You're the talk of the village!...'

'You consumptive baggage,' screamed Maria, 'that's outright slander and you know it! What, me with Hangman Thomas?'

'With Hangman Thomas!' sighed the old man down below, as he released the stone from the donkey's other flank. 'With Hangman Thomas!' And two tears rolled down his cheeks. 'I thought your family would show me compassion and defend me!... and I treated my nephews and nieces, my own flesh and blood, unjustly for your sake; but instead I get the same mockery from you as from everybody else!... Ah, ah! I made over everything I had to you, everything; and though under no obligation, I work for you from dawn to dusk, Maria, when I should be eating, drinking and taking life easy. Oh, what has become of me, what has become of me, fool that I am! So this is the solace that you promised me!'

'Just you wait till my Yannis gets back,' Maria was shouting at Chrysanthi threateningly, 'I'll tell him everything, yes everything. Ah, you wicked gossip, your mouth will turn to maggots. But we'll escape your clutches... I'd even work the streets in town to get away from you! That's right! How dare you even think of me with Hangman

Thomas! Who? Hangman Thomas?'

Suddenly the old man downstairs started laughing bitterly.

'Doesn't she know, ha, ha, ha!, doesn't that hussy Maria know I can revive old scores and make things hot for her, I can spell out her misdeeds down to the very last iota, both as a lass and as a married woman. Ha, ha, ha! Or perhaps she thinks I have forgotten? She'll come pleading soon enough, the way she did when she was after my property. Yes, indeed, Chrysanthi, you're quite right to accuse her. Yes, these old man's hands have fondled and caressed her. Ha, ha! Such stains never disappear with time ... Never! Ha, ha! Yes, both in my house and down in the hut at Fano. Call me nicknames all you like, Maria, but it was my shears that clipped your tail, ha, ha!'

'D'you hear? d'you hear?' Chrysanthi said to her spitefully, 'He's taking you to task in front of me. All those dirty secrets, eh, and acting holier than thou! Shame on you, you slut!'

'Viper!' screamed Maria, beside herself with rage.

Then she went over to the window and looked down, trying to spot the old man through the vine leaves rustling in the midday breeze.

'You dishonourable scoundrel, Hangman Thomas,' she said. 'How dare you slander me like this, you foul-mouthed wretch? Have you no fear of God, or of my husband? You've one foot in the grave already!' And thumping her palm with her fist she continued, 'I'm the one who's caught you in a sack* and bound you hand and foot, poor fellow! You thought you had everything so cleverly worked out, but all in vain ... Even if you swallow the cutlery to please me, I won't do you the favour, nor did I ever! Rant and carry on all day, it won't make any difference! You're in my hands, you wretch ... I've got you just where I want you. You can't even afford to pay for your own tombstone ... and I shall make your house into a seraglio for my children and my husband, long may he live. Any day you'll kick the bucket, because you're old and decrepit, Hangman Thomas, whereas we will go on living!'

'You too, you too,' he groaned and another tear rolled down his cheek.

'I refuse to be slandered just because of you,' she shouted.

He again began to laugh.

'Ha, ha, ha! You're right to feel ashamed and not want anyone to know the things we got up to, the things we still get up to ... Quite right! Justice is on your side. But "let not wrath come between man and wife, nor enmity between siblings", as the saying goes, ha, ha! And are we not man and wife? Aren't you my very own Maria? What else . . . We'll fall in love again and carry on as God intended . . . Yes, yes . . . Ha, ha! You're absolutely right!'

'You dishonourable scoundrel, Hangman Thomas!' she screamed again, trembling with fury. 'Just watch your mouth. When my husband gets back he'll give you the thrashing of your life. You're digging your own grave. I swear by the holy cross (she crossed herself), I'll never mate with you . . . Never, ever . . . I'll see you in Hell first . . . I don't deserve these insult, because I never did what you accuse me of . . . But you deserve to be punished, roasted alive for that slanderous tongue of yours. I won't even bring you water any more . . . I've no intention of giving people an excuse to gossip . . . You weren't content to live peaceably with us, instead you started getting ideas into your head! Are you listening? Well, don't get the idea you can back out of our agreement! No way, it's too late for that! If you want, stay on quietly and keep your mouth shut, otherwise when you're hungry or thirsty no one will attend to you, and when you fall ill we'll let you rot in bed the way you did to your poor wife. That's what you deserve. Yes indeed! What made you think women can be treated in this way? Don't you see how dearly you've paid for your obsession? Do you want to pay further? You make me sick . . . Shut up, shut up . . .'

And as she spoke she thumped her palm with her fist.

Just then Argyris entered the house, tall, stout, pale, out of breath and sweating profusely; he went over to the table and collapsed into a chair beside it, his legs outstretched before him. Maria quietened down at once, while Thomas continued answering back from down below, but Argyris, too angry and exhausted to say anything after struggling up the hill, just rolled his little eyes.

'Air, more air,' he whispered finally, unbuttoning his chest.

Chrysanthi hurried over to him anxiously, her head wobbling, tears in her eyes, and at once took off her headscarf and started fanning his face with it. Then glancing at Maria full of hatred, she said to her, 'Look what you've done, you hussy, look what you've done! God will make you pay for this. You'll be the death of my poor husband! . . .'

'You could be heard down in the square,' Argyris protested faintly. 'People were standing up to listen. What on earth's the matter now?

Have you no shame? And such foul language, it would disgrace a brothel! Each fanning the other's flames. I was obliged to come back up the hill at the double, and now look what you've done to me. I'm going to have a fit. May God repay you!'

'Such a vulgar brawl,' said Chrysanthi tearfully.

'Get stuffed!' replied Maria, gesturing obscenely at her with both hands and storming out.

Downstairs Thomas continued his grumbling. He had unloaded the donkey and was standing in front of the poor beast and gazing at it, as if hoping it might be able to protect him.

After a while Argyris recovered and, going over to the window, called down, 'Thomas, what d'you mean by raising merry hell and slandering my sister-in-law?'

'What else could I have expected from your confounded clan!' replied Thomas.

'You got some wicked ideas into your head . . .' Argyris called back. 'Forget about them, you're an old man now.'

'Ah, you've caught me in a sack, Maria told me so herself. If you're an honourable man, let's go and cancel our agreement. I don't want to be under your thumb. Let's call the whole thing off, Argyris! . . .'

'That can't be done,' replied Argyris with a smile. 'Have you gone a day without your food and drink, your washing, tidying up and pocket money? Am I to blame if you had other ideas and were not successful?'

He laughed and turning back into the room resumed his seat.

'Bring me something to eat, will you,' he said to Chrysanthi after a pause.

She obeyed at once. Argyris sat there alone for a while, listening to Thomas's resentful grumblings without responding.

Suddenly his brother and the priest came in, with Maria close on their heels. The priest had forgotten his grand manner and was pale, sweating and evidently in a towering rage. Yannis, in shirtsleeves and bare-chested, was smiling as usual with his eyes half closed, while Maria, still furious with Thomas, looked about her, nervously chewing at her headscarf.

'What's up, Reverend,' asked Argyris after greeting him, screwing up his little eyes.

'You won't believe this, Maria,' said the priest, talking rapidly and airing his skirts without so much as a good-day, 'it's quite outrageous, your father has taken leave of his senses. He's behaving like a little child. As you know, the authorities have revoked his licence, and quite rightly so. He couldn't see, he could no longer write because his hand shakes, no one can read the contracts he draws up, not even he himself, so how can he practice as a notary? Moreover, his affairs were in a muddle. And now what does he want? Since he's no longer practicing, he says, and can't afford to support his wife's bridesmaid, he wants — listen to this! — to bring her home to live with us. Yes, in our house... Think what an impossible position this puts me in... Am I, a priest, supposed to become a field-guard and take turns with my wife and family keeping watch lest he enthrone her in my home? Just think about it... I, a priest, and he expects me to cohabit with that whore... The whole thing is quite intolerable!... Quite intolerable!...'

'Goodness, what a slap in the face,' exclaimed Maria, tugging at her cheeks. 'Old age is certainly not without its problems...'

'He's on his way here now, so brace yourselves,' the priest continued.

'Ha, ha, ha!' laughed Thomas. 'It's his house, he can do what he likes with it. He has every right to. Ha, ha, ha!'

'Mind your own business, Hangman Thomas,' the priest shouted down angrily.

'It's the mullah!...' cried Thomas with a bitter laugh. 'The mullah, ha, ha!... and even he is calling people by their nicknames... He's forgotten that the bishop was reluctant to ordain him, because he thought him a cracked vessel!'

Meanwhile Yannis, his eyes half closed, was chuckling and saying, 'He too wants a bit of crumpet, and why not? Just because he's old? Ha, ha, ha!'

The priest gave him a sidelong glance and then continued, 'Now he's realised we don't want her, he's threatening to marry her. He thinks he can foist her onto us that way... But it's out of the question. How can I have that woman, a Jezebel like her, under the same roof as my own wife and daughters? A Jezebel like her... Absolutely not!... If he goes ahead with it, he'll find the door barred. You too should be prepared; nobody can ever say we're not completely justified. Nobody...'

'The Reverend's right,' said Maria gravely. 'What a day it's been...'

'Ha, ha!' Thomas could be heard laughing, 'so the notary's getting married. Ha, ha! Serve you all damn right.'

'Goodness, what a slap in the face,' Maria exclaimed again, 'the very stones must be rattling with laughter.'

'He'll be coming here to beg for your support,' said the priest, 'but pay no attention to him. I don't refuse him anything. He personally can have anything he wants, but as for his wife's bridesmaid, I don't want to know about her . . . Good-day to you.'

And with this he stormed angrily out of the house. Thomas laughed uproariously again.

'Allow me to handle things when he arrives,' Argyris said. 'But now let's eat.'

Here Maria too went out, while Yannis sat down beside his brother and the two of them proceeded to discuss their day-to-day affairs — the freshly ploughed field, the ripening olives, the bullock Yannis was to slaughter and the chapel the village was having built in the new cemetery. Argyris was one of the churchwardens. Finally the two women reappeared with the victuals, placed them on the table and returned to the kitchen to eat with their children. Yannis tucked in greedily, leaning over his thick plate and slurping with his lips, while Argyris took his time, putting dainty morsels in his mouth and wheezing continually. Neither brother spoke. Finally Argyris remarked, 'I wish I had your appetite, you know, Yannis. That's what being free of worries does for one . . . Would you still be like that, going it alone?'

'Alone?' said Yannis laughing. 'But I have no such plans. Maria talks about it, but so what? Who listens to his wife? Ha, ha!'

After that they finished their meal in silence.

'Here comes the notary,' observed Argyris a moment later with a smile, and got up ready to receive him.

Tall, stooping and emaciated, with hollow temples and hectic hollow cheeks, the old man entered and greeted them in his faint voice. His lively eyes were yellowish and restless, but his red lips appeared to be smiling.

Maria had followed him in.

'Ah, your Honour . . .' said Argyris.

'Welcome, father,' said Yannis.

'Will you have a bite to eat?' Argyris asked him.

'No,' he replied in his frail voice, 'I've not eaten but I don't feel up to it. Not when she is going hungry!'

And he shook his head ruefully as he said this.

Everyone pretended not to hear and the notary began again, smiling his involuntary smile as his gaze wandered restlessly about the room.

'Our village is a wicked place, my children, it's another Sodom! And why doesn't God send down fire to burn it? To avoid setting the churches, which are Orthodox, on fire as well.* Ah, what have I done to deserve such calumny from people? Why should they complain to the Public Prosecutor, putting him to the expense of coming from town by coach to review my practice? He made me read the documents I'd drafted, but I couldn't make them out because my old specs are no use, and even he, an educated man, couldn't make head nor tail of them, being unaccustomed to my handwriting. And then he found my certificate was not in order, because in Athens they change the regulations every day... and that gave him a pretext to confiscate my licence and close me down... And now...'

'Now?' said Maria.

'Now... now... now... I don't get any business... not even enough to pay for a loaf of bread a day... So what am I to take her? She will starve to death.'

'Take whom?' asked Maria casually.

The old man looked nervously about and his hectic cheeks perspired a little, but the smile still lingered on his lips. He was afraid of mentioning the woman's name, as if it were obscene, but finally he took the plunge: 'My wife's bridesmaid!' he said, lowering his restless eyes.

'Oh, her,' said Maria with contempt. 'Pah!'

'But Maria,' pleaded the old man, 'what's she ever asked of me, a crust of bread to keep body and soul together... The priest and your sister have refused, because they say she's not my wife! We're not related. Oh, that priest, that priest... Devil take his soul. And your sister, my curse upon her too! Now they've put me on the street! Because how am I to eat and drink while the woman who's grown old with me goes hungry? Oh God, procure my rights!... And I told them I'd marry her and could then bring her back as my lawful wedded wife, to what is still after all my house... But they refused... They've hurt me to the core and now I go about cursing them and sighing... No good will come to the priest's wife... My grandchildren will die on her; God will grieve her as bitterly as she's grieved me...' And the tears ran down his hollow cheeks.

'Oh, if my wife's bridesmaid were a wealthy woman,' he continued after a pause, 'if she had property and money, you'd see how keen they'd be to have her, you'd see . . .'

'Father,' Maria interrupted him, 'come to your senses and don't ask a priest for the impossible, don't make yourself ridiculous in your old age.'

'Maria,' he replied trembling, 'you're a good girl, may God bless you, and you respect me in old age, you'll be happy here together with your husband and your children! Surely you're not going to embitter your old father too. You're not going to throw me out like the priest, or refuse the crust of bread I beg in charity for that poor woman . . . You're not going to behave like the priest's wife . . . You won't forget how in times of misery and hardship after your mother died that woman held our family together, saw to all your needs, loved you like a mother . . . She beggared herself for our sake by selling her own home lest it be said that we were selling ours! . . . And at least when she's my wife, you won't let her starve to death, because you are a kind-hearted person, God bless you and your children!'

And he again began to weep.

'Ha, ha, ha!' laughed Thomas from below, 'the notary's getting married, and so young, eighty years old if he's a day! And he's begging his daughter for a crust to boost his strength! Ha, ha! The bridal pair are feeling peckish before producing babies! Ha, ha! Your Honour, two madmen have come together here . . . We've both given away our possessions to your daughter! Ha, ha.'

Here Yannis interjected, 'He's not asking us for much, Maria . . . After all we have his land . . . He could have sold it if he'd wanted!'

The notary gave him an appreciative look, but Maria now lost patience. 'Father,' she said, 'for your own good forget about that woman; she's the one who ruined you. Today you'd be an important man awash with money if it weren't for her! Give her up and stop worrying about her. She'll survive, no one on the island has ever starved to death. Go home, and the priest and his wife will receive you as your children. Go home alone and don't do the wicked thing you're contemplating. We're all ashamed of her.'

'I see!' exclaimed the notary, trembling from head to foot and staring at her, though his pallid lips continued to smile involuntarily, 'I see!'

Here Argyris said to him earnestly, 'Neither the priest's wife nor Maria has any obligation to that woman. As things stand they can't acknowledge her, and if you marry her they still won't do so, because they are ashamed of her. So it would not be wise, your Honour.'

'Oh, my curse upon the pack of you . . .' he replied. 'Argyris, you're behind this . . . It was all your scheme, you greedy scoundrel.'

He got up, tottered to the door and stepped out into the road.

'My curse on you, Maria . . .' he continued, as he set off down the hill. 'Argyris delivered you into the hands of Hangman Thomas so he could secure his house and land; but your family will also rue the day . . .'

And as he hurried down the hill, tears kept welling in his eyes.

'I shall go begging for a crust to keep my wife and me alive,' he muttered, 'but will strangers be any more compassionate? . . .'

Thomas watched him leave, following him with his gaze, and then burst out laughing: 'Ha, ha, ha! One madman has departed, the other remains here with his donkey.'

Then, dragging the beast by its halter, he strode towards his house. But as he went he was suddenly overcome by a heart-wrenching fit of sobbing and, abandoning the donkey, he flung himself face down upon his bed.

'Oh, Maria, Maria . . . both me and your own father, why have you poisoned both our lives like this? Oh, Maria, Maria, Maria!'

And he wept, and wept.

# X

Spring, the season of work, had again returned and it was midday. In the village the shops and houses were all shut, very few people were about in the main street and not a sound came from the animals. Everyone in Argyris's house was out that day, as there was work to be seen to in the fields and olives to be gathered that the recent storm had scattered on the ground.

Only Maria was at home. She had remained behind to cook for those out labouring in the fields. She now gave the stew one final stir, ladled some out, raised it to her lips, blew on it and tasted it, and deciding it was ready unhooked the large black pot from the iron tripod.

'I might as well give Thomas his share first,' she said to herself, taking a thick plate down from the shelf and filling it with reddish stew. Then she cut a large slice of bread, tucked it under her arm and left the kitchen carrying the plate.

But today she did not as usual leave it on Thomas's step and knock to let him know, but went straight on in, calling out his name. There she found him sitting pensively on his old chest. She smiled and greeted him. It was the first time she had addressed a word to him since the day of their quarrel.

'Welcome, my dear,' exclaimed the old man when he saw her, 'come in, come in!'

And his whole face lit up with joy. He was on his feet in a jiffy and, taking the plate and bread from her, he added, 'Let me help you, give it here, I'll put it on the chest.' He stood there before her a few seconds, gazing at her passionately, then glanced toward the door, as if calculating whether he would have time to block her retreat.

'You see the way things are, Thomas,' she now said to him. 'People are malicious and spread wicked rumours; you know how that viper carries on in here.'

'I'll pluck her eyes out for you, shall I?' he said flushing.

'That's not what I came about. In fact I'd sworn never to speak to you again. You were far too forward . . . and as you know, I don't like such embarrassing scenes. What happened, happened, but don't try to overstep the mark again. People's tongues have to stop wagging. I allowed you your little pranks occasionally because I thought of you as an elder, as my father, but pranks are one thing and serious matters quite another. So if you want us to live in harmony, make up your mind to it, settle down and stop your monstrous behaviour, or else you'll be the one to suffer.'

'Oh, Maria...' he sighed with tears in his eyes.

'The worst of it is, I don't know how to behave towards you. If I abuse you, people condemn me because your property is in our hands; if I'm kind to you, they slander us and you quickly take advantage, then...'

'Ever since that day,' he reproached her bitterly, 'you've all been mocking me. You yourself now use my nickname all the time, you've given your children free reign to taunt me, and every one of them now bursts out laughing when I lose my temper. What a misery all of you have made my life... You show no compassion! Have you no pity?' And he heaved a deep resentful sigh. 'How can I go on living like this?'

'You go around saying such things in all the wine-stores and people turn against us, you give us a bad name.'

'What else do you expect?' he sighed defensively.

'Yesterday we were summoned by Lord Argyris, who gave us all a dressing down and cursed me soundly; that viper told him I encourage the children to tease you and to use your nickname. And if I did, it was only because you embarrassed me at every turn. I don't want people thinking you really are my lover and that's how I got you to hand over your property, because I want everyone to know I love my husband. He's such a good man, God bless him, and so manly... But people, as I say, have tongues and gossip, even though you're old... especially when you yourself go about spreading wicked rumours.'

'You've been tormenting me, Maria,' he said plaintively. 'What have you ever asked that I've not done for you? I've been willing to work like a coolie, like a slave for you, scot free... But what was it you promised, what was our little understanding? Then once I'd signed the deeds, you suddenly changed your tune and turned against me; and now you won't spend a single moment in my company, whether in secret or in public, not a single moment. And your children, ah me, I'm hounded by them too. Even your younger daughter Olga, the things she puts me through...'

She looked at him with sympathy a moment, and said with a coy smile, 'Poor Thomas!'

Mollified a little, Thomas's face lit up at once and he sighed and gazed at Maria for a moment, a tear in his eye.

'As for my Olga,' said Maria, 'I don't believe it, she's the one who feels sorry for you and weeps when the others make you angry.'

'She's the worst... worse even than Chrysanthi, who makes you behave so brutally to me. The little minx, she always enters timidly with honeyed words, and never swears or calls me by my nickname, but she knows full well that she's to blame and that's why she's afraid of me. Her sympathy is all hypocrisy and lies, even if she's still only a girl. How come you've brought her up like this, Maria, and how will she turn out when ripe, God damn her! Whenever she's the one who brings my food, it's quite inedible — so peppery it would drive a dog insane, no dressing on the greens, full of dirt and hairs, lice swimming in the coffee even! ... She does all this to starve me, but one of these days I'll give her a good hiding, so don't say I haven't warned you. Yet she approaches me so sweetly that I'm taken in afresh each time. What's she do it for, Maria? She even brought me a dung-filled cigarette! Ah, the little ...'

'The children,' she said thoughtfully, 'sense what it is you want from me and that's why they resent you. And they're right, because you're determined to bring shame on us. But I can't believe this of my Olga. Andreas must have put her up to it; he and Amalia invent ways to provoke you, then send the little one while they look on and laugh.'

She laughed.

'So you think it's funny too?' he said, suddenly flaring up again. 'And when you see them at it, you feel proud of them, eh? But I can laugh as well, we'll soon see who has the last laugh ...'

Meanwhile he had managed to get between her and the door, blocking her exit. Then suddenly, when Maria was least expecting it, he seized her round the waist with his strong hands and tightening his grip tried to push her towards the bed.

'Though you fly to the bosom of the Lord,' he cried, 'you shan't escape me. No, you shan't escape me.'

And he tried to kiss her.

She reacted immediately and stepping sideways, herself began pushing Thomas back towards the door, holding her head away from his face to avoid his kiss and glaring at him, crimson with rage. Then thrusting one hand against his forehead, she forced his head back with all her might, while with the other arm clamped across her breast she tried to keep him as far away from her as possible. And through clenched teeth she hissed at him with hatred, 'Thomas, let go or I'll scream! Let go of me, I say!'

And she continued to struggle and resist him.

'Do what you like,' he replied kissing her hand with a demonic laugh. 'There's no one about! And I have my rights. That was our little understanding when you took my property.'

Bracing one leg, he managed to force her another step back towards the bed, then with the blood rushing to his face he paused to catch his breath before making a renewed attempt. For a moment she felt her strength failing and feared the old man would get the better of her; her heart pounded, her face changed colour and beads of sweat poured from her brow; but with her hand still thrust against his forehead she kept jerking and twisting his head back, while trying with the other elbow to poke him in the chest; and to avoid finding herself prostrate on the bed should he manage to force her back another step, she struggled with all her might to turn him round, gritting her teeth, panting for breath and by now thoroughly alarmed.

Taking two steps sideways, he managed to push her back a little further and she realized that she was in real peril. At any moment he would overpower her and have her sprawling on the bed. This induced her to redoubled her efforts. Her face turning purple, she shook him violently and baring her white teeth flecked with spume she glared at him and hissed, 'You scoundrel, Hangman Thomas, no, no! I won't do you the favour! I'll see you in Hell first.'

And for an instant she let go his forehead. He chuckled, thinking he had won. But quick as a flash she grabbed him by the throat and squeezed and twisted his scrawny gullet with her strong fingers.

'I'll show you, you scoundrel!'

Struggling to escape her grasp, the old man twisted his torso this way and that, took first one then two more steps back, managed to swing her round to the side of the bed again, only to find himself hurtling towards the door with her, tried to shake free, jerking his head back, then tightening his grip brought her round into the middle of the room, but still she would not let go. He felt a sharp pain in his neck and had difficulty breathing, his veins bulged with arrested blood, turning his face blue, his eyes started from their sockets, his ears buzzed and his skull felt ready to explode, so that instinctively he let go of Maria's waist with one hand to grapple with the hand choking him. This gave her greater freedom to manoeuvre and without letting go his throat, she thrust him backwards with all her might and suddenly managed to free herself from his grasp, while Thomas went sprawling back against the chest. Maria sprang to safety by the door and, panting after the struggle and elated by her victory, paused to look back at him. He was now sitting exhausted, in pain and out of breath, his head bowed in shame and struggling to swallow the saliva in his gullet.

'You scoundrel, Hangman Thomas,' she cursed him, 'didn't I tell you not to try it on with me, even in jest?'

The old man started trembling all over; that confounded nickname again made him see red, the more so since he was unable to respond at once and let off steam, being completely out of breath.

'I'll cook your goose, Hangman Thomas,' she said maliciously. 'I'll see you rot!'

He was considering whether he might not grab hold of her again. Swallowing dryly a couple of times, he looked her straight in the eyes and said bitterly, 'Hangman Thomas, eh? After you've fleeced me, eh?'

He fingered and rubbed his aching neck. Then quite unexpectedly he laughed and said to her good-humouredly, 'Once upon a time, lame Asimina, Spatharos's wife, poisoned her lover and committed seven other murders in our village. When they reached a verdict she was bound hand and foot to the tails of four horses, stark naked, her shame exposed to the sun. The horses tore her into four quarters, which were buried at the four corners of the village, and the crosses stand there as a warning to this day.* You have the same twisted soul, Maria; that hallowed law ought still to be in force and the same thing done to you . . .' He sighed. 'Why are you so evil?'

'I don't want you, you disgusting old tramp. May you burst with frustration, Hangman Thomas, I spit on you.' And she spat.

All at once the old man started weeping mournfully, large tears rolling down his cheeks as he said plaintively, 'You too, Maria, you too have turned against me, just like all the others, you too are driving me to desperate measures . . . You knew I was old, you knew how much I loved you, and you've beggared me . . . You coaxed and wheedled until you had me in your power, and now you despise me, curse me and torment me. Hangman Thomas, eh? The children from the ridge-tops in the morning, the village women in the evening, your brats from dawn to dusk and now you too ... And not the slightest gratitude. Ah, life is not worth living, I can't go on like this ...' And he rapped his head hard with his fist.

Suddenly her rage abated and she looked at him compassionately, forgetting for an instant all he'd done to her and feeling her heart softening towards him. 'Poor wretch ...' she said.

Thomas looked at her dolefully for a while with tears in his eyes, as if begging her for mercy, then at last he said, 'Oh, Maria, one word from you, a single "yes", would grant me a taste of Paradise on earth ... Would that I were young again, if only for a minute before I kick the bucket ... Oh, you would desire me then ... But like this, the way I am?'

She laughed at first but then became indignant: 'Don't you realize what you're asking? Can't you see what a manly husband I have and how much I love him?'

'And our little agreement?' he said looking down bashfully.

She did not reply. Then suddenly Thomas's eyes dried and sparkled with resentment, and flaring up he said to her with malice, 'I shall be your enemy and the enemy of your family and children ... I shall wish you ill and seek to do you harm, because you've cheated me. I want to cancel the life annuity agreement.'

'Oh, that can't be cancelled, Hangman Thomas,' she said mockingly, 'no, that can't be done.'

And she wagged the inverted fingers of one hand under her chin.

Now he no longer knew what he was saying to her: 'Hangman Thomas, eh? My name is Hangman Thomas, eh? You've forgotten, it seems, what happened years ago when you were a young lass, still almost a girl. I had a donkey then as well and every day I'd ride past my olive trees not far from my hut. Don't blush, Maria! There's no denying it ... There you were, half naked with your cousin in a ditch. Ha, ha, ha! ... just like Amalia with Andreas now, God bless them! The number of times I've seen those two together, and they no longer even feel ashamed! Ha, ha, ha! Indeed, I have encouraged them, as I enjoy seeing all of you disgraced ... It was the same with you ... Your cousin took to his heels and is still running ... I leaped into the ditch and very nearly caught you, and you'd have enjoyed it too, as I was still young in those days, although already married . . . But your headscarf was all I managed to grab hold of. You scurried off home bare-headed and I hung it like a banner from a tree outside my hut for all to see; later your mother came to retrieve it from my wife and they both cursed you soundly . . . Now you've learned to swear yourself of course . . . How come you've forgotten all of that?'

'Ah, Hangman Thomas . . .' she said with hatred.

'You started whoring at an early age, just like your daughter!'

'I must be mad to stand here listening to you . . . The whole family is waiting for me in the field; God damn you, Hangman Thomas, see how you've delayed me . . .' She started to go, but was so furious she couldn't tear herself away. 'Hangman Thomas,' she shouted from the yard, 'you're an evil man, plain evil! What do you expect to do with what you've told me, you dirty old man, no one will believe you! Just leave my daughter alone and stop spying on her, do you hear! And may you eat your envious heart out sitting there in silence, because we'll be making love upstairs deliberately, to torture you.'

'She claims she loves her husband,' laughed Thomas, pointing at her with his finger, 'yet she cheats him too! I know everything and can give you all the details, all of them! . . .'

Rage now took complete possession of her, the blood rose to her cheeks and she rushed back inside preparing to strike him, but the old man only looked at her mockingly and laughed.

'You just watch it, Hangman Thomas,' she said fuming, 'or I'll fetch an axe and chop your head off, just like John the Baptist.* Shame on you, shame, I spit on you!'

And she shook her finger threateningly and spat. He opened his large hands in lewd invitation. Her fury now boiled over uncontrollably. Suddenly she started screaming like a madwoman, 'Hangman Thomas is trying to rape me! Hangman Thomas . . .'

This alarmed the old man and he rose from the chest and looked round apprehensively, but carried away by the sudden surge of emotion he went on laughing with tears in his eyes. Meanwhile Maria, choking with rage and no longer conscious of what she was doing, suddenly lifted her skirt in front of him, tucking it under her chin to leave both hands free.

And standing there with her arms akimbo displaying her nakedness before him, her eyes ablaze with hatred and spittle on her lips, she said, 'Here I am, here I am, naked before you! I'm not ashamed, Hangman Thomas, you scoundrel, because you're old! Look, look! I'm saving my body for my virile young husband to enjoy, that's right, you pathetic creature! Eat your heart out with frustration!'

And letting her skirts fall, she leaned forward and spat directly in his face.

The old man blanched, stopped laughing and began to tremble; then pitching forward, first onto his knees and then full length onto the ground, he buried his face in his arms and began to weep.

Maria had by now gone back out into the yard and from there continued screaming, 'Neighbours, come quickly, run, Hangman Thomas is trying to rape me!'

Soon quite a crowd had gathered, men, women and children, all laughing and cursing and denouncing Hangman Thomas, all eager to know every last detail of what had taken place. One woman was saying to Maria, 'You should have scratched that Hangman Thomas's eyes out!'

'I told you so,' another said. 'He had ulterior motives when he entered into that life annuity agreement.'

'He found plenty to amuse him, dirty old man,' observed a third.

'An elderly man and he stoops to that!' muttered one old codger.

'Argyris ought to turn him out of the house,' someone else exclaimed.

'Lucky you escaped,' still others told her. 'No one has any sympathy for him.'

And the children, laughing as they waited outside Thomas's door for him to emerge, started shouting, 'Boo, boo, Hangman Thomas . . . Boo, boo, Hangman Thomas . . .'

The old man had by this time risen from the floor and was sitting on his ancient chest in silence, his hands clasped together anxiously, uncertain how to extricate himself from this hellish situation, and now and then a tear would trickle down his cheek. His humiliating nickname repeatedly assailed his ears like a violent whiplash.

At this point Maria's husband too appeared among the crowd

Feeling hungry, he had left the others working in the field and returned to find out why his wife had not come down. Seeing so many people outside his home, he smilingly enquired what was going on and with half-closed eyes listened as his wife explained, with much shouting and gesticulation, that Thomas had rushed at her and tried to rape her.

The crowd listened with bated breath to what she had to say. Many of them threatened Thomas, and the children went on mocking him. But Yannis burst out laughing uncontrollably and said, 'Is that all it was? But he's so old, what could he have done?'

And he went on into the kitchen to relieve his hunger. But Maria, determined to provoke her husband, shouted angrily from the yard, 'That scoundrel Hangman Thomas isn't as weak as you might think; he was within an ace of overturning me onto his bed and making you a cuckold, my poor Yannis. Go on, pretend to be indifferent . . .'

Just then Argyris appeared among the crowd, tall, stout, pale and out of breath, his big stick in his hand, closely followed by the notary, stooping, wrinkled, rosy-lipped, his lively restless eyes now full of curiosity. Argyris instantly grasped what was afoot and went straight into Thomas's house.

The old man rose from the chest in a daze, looked about as if seeking some protection, and blushing deeply said in a hoarse trembling voice, 'Ah, Argyris, let's cancel the life annuity arrangement.'

'It can't be cancelled,' said Argyris gravely in his ugly falsetto, trying hard to smile. 'It can't be cancelled . . . We've now invested too much money in your property! . . . But why are you dissatisfied? Your food and drink, your clothing, your domestic chores are all taken care of, aren't they? But you have other things in mind, eh? Ah well, we can't oblige you there . . . No, we can't oblige you there . . .'

And chuckling to himself he stepped outside again.

The crowd meanwhile had begun to disperse in a good mood. Argyris overheard the notary saying to people in his weak quavering voice, 'I thought my curse had taken hold and someone must have died here, Argyris or my son-in-law or perhaps one of the children, so I rushed up here to see. No, no, don't listen to them: until we'd secured his property, my daughter was keen enough to have him; she was following Argyris's advice, God damn his father! Now they're doing all this to him to get him out of his own house and enjoy it unencumbered . . . My son-in-law and daughter did the same to me, and now I have to go begging for a crust to feed my wife . . . Yes, I married her. But my daughter and her husband won't let me bring her home . . . They don't want us . . . The priest, confound him, and Argyris are responsible for everything. I pray to God that not a soul among them lives, that my grandchildren all perish!'

And with this the old man set off down the hill again, mingling with the laughing crowd and ignoring Argyris who called out to him from his front door.

# XI

Months had passed and one morning Thomas got out of bed in a foul mood and, his eyes bulging, suddenly yelled out, 'I'll become a fiend!'*

And with his head bowed he began to pace restlessly about the room, despair written on his aged ruddy face.

'Ah, I'll become altogether evil!' he went on. 'The whole village is to blame, everyone, everyone . . . I'm a martyr on this earth, they all hate me, I'm the village laughing-stock . . . A buffoon. Ah God! It's Hangman Thomas this, Hangman Thomas that, even Maria now calls me Hangman Thomas . . . Even Maria . . . The women every evening, the people in the village, the children on the ridge-tops . . . Even Maria . . .'

And as he said this, he felt utterly heartsick and dejected and longed to do something that would release him from frustration, make him terrible to others and ease his insatiable passion; and as he continued pacing and grinding his few teeth, he would close his eyes tight, as if to picture in his imagination what he might do, then open them again in fright, or pause and sigh, or glower at the heavens in despair. He even thought about his late wife, her death, their life together and his vanished youth. Who would have dared to tease him in his prime? Everyone had known he could turn nasty if provoked; human beings fear one another, that's the only reason they don't devour each other like the wolves . . . But now they all considered him weak and ineffectual, that was why they were harassing him, they always picked on the elderly, on unfortunate old codgers like himself . . . His sister had warned him and she'd been right. Old people, she had said, are better off dead. And he reflected that most people of his age were already lying in their graves at peace, and no longer had to suffer the bitterness and malice of this world; but then suddenly he felt afraid of death, of dark and chilly Hades, of the endless sleep with no awakening that grips a man relentlessly, however much he might resist, freezing him by slow degrees and depriving him of breath, plunging him into who knows what uncharted terrifying worlds, or into nothingness perhaps . . . His despair became intolerable, for he could find salvation neither in his heart nor in the world around him, and the poison of envy took possession of his soul. Others were surrounded by the smiling faces of their loved ones and could satisfy their longing for affection. Even Argyris, that malicious fellow, despite his ailments, even the notary, despite the poverty and wretchedness of his existence! And Yannis? Ah, Yannis enjoyed every imaginable happiness... And countless other people too, everywhere he looked; admittedly sadness and distress were widespread, but life had a sweet smile, or amorous sigh, or act of charity reserved for everyone; he alone in the whole village was orphaned, hated and forlorn! Everyone else was able to enjoy life and forget the bitterness of death; he alone was forced to contemplate his end and wrestle incessantly with Charon, because his life had become as poisonous as death itself.

'Poisonous! Poisonous!' he sighed.

Anger stirred within him. 'At least let others have a taste of grief as well!' he muttered. They would always suffer less than him, much less! But their harm would give him satisfaction and gladden his poor heart, especially if it afflicted those who'd wronged him, but anybody else as well: if they were human beings then they were his enemies. In such an unjust world kindness received no reward, nor would crimes be punished... He was not such a fool as to believe the fairytales dished out by priests... He knew full well why they talked the way they did... He could see for himself how they behaved; he need look no further than Maria's brother-in-law, that greedy fellow, who had made an old man's life a misery while himself enjoying wife, family and wealth, who cheated innocent folk with the fear of death and Hell, preaching penitence and love, the hypocrite! Everywhere injustice reigned! That was why he too was determined to wreak havoc.

'I'll become a fiend,' he declared again, 'a fiend...'

His mind moved swiftly on to other things. Argyris's neighbour kept two enormous oxen down at his hut... He was a good man and had never called him by his nickname; he lived quietly with his poor family, bent all day over his labour, watering the earth with his sweat, unfailingly cheerful!... Why should this man live happily, while he himself had such a wretched life? Oh, at that moment he hated him as well, simply because he was a human being and humanity had wronged him... He wanted misfortune to befall him too. The huge oxen would now be resting peacefully beneath the olive trees: if only he could destroy them and watch him also suffer... That at least was one of life's pleasures he could enjoy... The neighbour would shed tears and beat his chest ... with the oxen lying there prostrate out on the ground ... He would call on him, Thomas, for assistance, Thomas the despised ... Ha, ha, ha! he chuckled. A few needles mixed in with their fodder, and two or three months later the oxen would be dead.

He felt capable of far greater infamy than this, of every conceivable abomination, yes he, Thomas the weakling, Thomas the despised ... He would declare war on society at large and come away unscathed ... A veritable fiend ... Why stop at the neighbour, why not wreak vengeance on that grasping swine Argyris, and on Maria too? The things she'd made him suffer ... What about Yannis then, Yannis was different, he was not malicious ... But doesn't God send earthquakes, floods and lightning that destroy the just and the unjust alike? Thomas would do likewise ... Let his schemes harm Yannis too ... But then again, how much power did he really have, forlorn and persecuted as he was, daily stooping closer to the earth under the burden of his woes?

He sighed, then promptly laughed: 'Ha, ha! God has blessed man with intelligence! The ox is directed by a little boy, the horse controlled with a mere bit and bridle ... And Thomas will manipulate you likewise, yes Thomas ... So far, kindness and generosity had failed to get him anywhere, might evil now bring some belated happiness? ... Thomas will be a veritable fiend ... Then they'll have every right to call him Hangman Thomas, Thomas the executioner, that is, and he won't resent it ... Or will he? Hmm! ... Hmm! ...'

Thereupon he left the house and, keeping his head well down, crept across to the garden shed where he kept his donkey tethered. The patient beast was resting on the ground, and on seeing him got to its feet awkwardly and looked at him.

'Argyris, you wretch,' he said (he had taken to calling it this some time ago), 'haven't you dropped dead yet, God damn your father.'

He tossed it an armful of hay from the corner of the shed.

'Here's something for you too, you poor old thing,' he continued. 'You're all I have left in the world, you're the only one who pays attention to me ...'

Then he grabbed another fistful of hay and, smiling satanically, returned to the house. There he opened the old black chest, still full of his wife's clothes, and rummaging among her things eventually found a little piece of cloth pierced with rusty needles. He sat down in the middle of the floor and one by one threaded them carefully through bits of straw. 'These should put paid to the good neighbour's oxen,' he said to himself. 'They'll swallow them down and in three months they'll be dead, for all their monstrous size!' And he sighed, disturbed by his own malice.

Then he got up and with the same satanic smile rummaged through the old clothes again, thrusting his hand to the very bottom of the chest until he found a small white pouch. He unfastened it with care. It contained a quantity of tiny yellow seeds. 'I knew they'd come in handy some day!' he said to himself. 'I gathered them last summer on the off chance. There must be over a thousand seeds here and they'll all take root! That's what makes tares unique. They're said to have the Devil's blessing, because their roots reach down several feet, poisoning the soil. They will take root in Argyris's vineyard in a month or so, and I shall laugh to see him rage when he has to write the harvest off.' In his mind's eye he could see the splendid vineyard with its vines flourishing all along the sun-drenched slope, and just now laden with succulent black grapes awaiting the harvester's pruning-knife. Suddenly Thomas became enraged. 'Ah, no!' he said savagely, 'even this year they shan't harvest them. I'll go down every row with a gorse switch and won't leave a single grape, not one! It will be worse than a hailstorm striking!* Then they'll see if Thomas's hatred is to be taken seriously and Maria too will learn her lesson! Maria who has grieved me so and cheated me, yes, cheated me . . .'

And he began to laugh and cry by turns.

Just then he heard Olga's voice calling from the yard. Instinctively he hid the seeds in his large palm, hastily locked the chest and went angrily over to the door.

'What d'you want, brat?' he said to her with hatred.

Then seeing her look down tearfully, he glared at her with angry bloodshot eyes and snarled, exposing his few remaining teeth: 'Think I've forgotten, eh! You're the one who's been plaguing me the most, acting the innocent with all your false humility. The food you bring me is so peppery it's unfit to eat, there are lice swimming in the coffee and you've even brought me dung-filled cigarettes! You're in league with the other two and they send you to do the dirty work. But I'll cripple you if you don't watch out!'

'Who, me, uncle Thomas,' she said plaintively, 'but I always take your side!'

She was on the brink of tears.

'Clear off!' the old man shouted, consumed with hatred.

'Andreas told me . . .' she murmured with a sigh.

'Clear off, you little minx,' he yelled again, itching to lay into her.

Just then Andreas appeared behind her, straight-faced but with a twinkle in his eye and evidently trying to restrain his laughter.

'Go on, off with you!' he told her, pretending to be annoyed. 'Thomas is right . . . he's always right.'

The young girl looked at him reproachfully and hurried away in tears.

'Thomas,' the lad continued, 'I've come to get your donkey; we're bringing in some corn we harvested this morning.'

'Let's go down together then!' replied Thomas smiling at him.

While Andreas led the donkey out of the shed and saddled it, the old man concealed the pouch full of seeds and the straw laced with needles in its nosebag and then locked up the house. Soon the two of them were on the road, Thomas astride his little beast and Andreas on foot beside him, and as they went they talked. Just then the old man was saying, 'You'd have an experienced person to consult, my lad, and your life would be transformed. Of course it would! But even you set out to provoke me, lad, with all your pranks and nicknames, and if you don't, you let the little ones be as cheeky as they please and laugh along with them . . .'

'Who, me!' said Andreas hypocritically, trying to suppress a smile and giving the donkey's rump a hearty smack.

'Yes, you and Amalia too! Whereas you, lad, should be advising Amalia to keep the little ones in check because, you know, I have both your interests at heart and could become your confidant and keep an eye out for you, then you could lead a life of bliss together.'

And as he said this he gave him a sly look. Andreas laughed out loud.

'Giddy-up!' he shouted to the donkey.

'If I were young,' Thomas went on, 'and had such a scrumptious cousin, I wouldn't let her slip through my fingers, only to have someone else take her away from me tomorrow! That would be stupid! You don't yet know what a woman is! A creature sweet as honey! Just like in the song! And Amalia's a little sweetie, made for you; yes, you're doing the right thing, and who can blame you? I'd go further, I'd treat her as my wife, because I wouldn't want to get consumption! Why risk that, and you'd be doing her a favour too. I'm an old man now, I've talked to people of all sorts, my inferiors and betters, and I know a thing or two, I dare say more than you! The root cause of consumption is frustrated love, my boy. Young fellows fall in love and then don't follow nature's urges; they let their bodies waste away with yearning, and so become consumptive and end up in an early grave ... And then the girls forget all about them, go dancing and get married. So take care you don't become consumptive too, you're thin enough already and it would be a shame ... You love her, don't you? Then don't listen to what old women and those rascally priests will tell you ... Indeed, they say the Synod has come up with a new ruling that cousins may get married ... On the other hand, why not bed her outside marriage? Not a bad idea either; in a year or two no one will be getting married anyway ... Besides, with Amalia you don't run any risk, none at all ... What can they to do to you? Is her father going to kill you, are her little brothers?* Ha, ha! You'll be sleeping in the same bed you sleep in now, except with her ... That's the only difference ... But what a difference, eh? Just think about it for a moment ... Ha, ha, ha! And you say I don't have your welfare at heart, what, me? ... Your father will shout and carry on a bit, but he'll probably shy away from trouble as he's a sick man; and your uncle Yannis will just laugh, that's all he ever does, we know him ... Her mother, Maria, is cantankerous and will raise merry hell, that's her nature, but who bothers about what women think ... Let them carry on ... People only laugh at them. At least words don't open mortal wounds. Let her curse and make a fuss, you'll just laugh it off and continue to enjoy her daughter. No skin off your nose ... And before you know it they'll need you for the harvest and come begging ... Listen: as this is how things stand, make her your mistress and curse me if that's not sound advice ... The sooner the better. We'll be meeting her down there in a little while, so make up your mind to it.'

Andreas listened to him earnestly with downcast eyes and forgot to beat the donkey.

'It's true,' he said blushing, 'I do love Amalia.'

'You think I don't know that, my boy?' he replied at once. 'I've seen the way you carry on together often enough. Why d'you think I'm telling you all this? If only I were young and she my cousin, you'd soon see... Get inside her knickers and have done with it, my lad! Otherwise sooner or later someone else will snap her up, and then you'll pine away and get consumption, no doubt about it, mark my word.'

'I do love her,' Andreas repeated involuntarily.

He could feel the old man's words kindling an irrepressible desire within him, like a searing flame, clouding his mind. With Amalia he would experience life quite differently, the old man was right in his advice, why hesitate, why let her slip through his fingers since he was the first to fall in love with her? And besides, how beautiful Amalia was... He could already imagine himself lying beside her, drawing her close with all the trembling ardour of his passion. In her embrace he would soon have his first taste of the new wine of life, the untried joys of sensual pleasure; he'd enjoy and teach her the intoxication of love that can eclipse the mind...

'You see?' said Thomas craftily, and chuckled.

'Yes, yes,' replied Andreas, as in a dream.

Then the two hurried on in silence down a slope that led through a grove of massive olive trees, their boughs splitting under the weight of their bounteous crop. The donkey picked its way cautiously down the rough path, and occasionally the old man would shout at it and whack it, glancing round slyly at Andreas who followed in a daze, and smiling to himself with satisfaction. For the first time he was savouring the sweetness of revenge. His rage was beginning to subside. Now it was his turn to make Maria suffer and he would laugh at her outrage and despair. Had life reserved some consolation, joy and happiness for him after all?

They were now approaching the hut and as they did so passed by the neighbour's dwelling. His two enormous oxen were lying resting under a large olive tree, tossing their heads to shake off the flies. Thomas looked at them maliciously for a moment and shook his own head at them aggressively.

Further on, stretching all across the hillside, was Argyris's dazzling green vineyard laden with black grapes, and where it ended on a patch of level ground stood the hut, while in the fertile valley at the bottom of the hill, several women were at work harvesting the corn. Thomas drew the youth's attention to them, saying, 'D'you see her... She's down there...' Then he dismounted.

'Yes,' replied Andreas blushing, and his eyes sparkled.

'If you bring her up here,' he told him in an undertone, 'I'll lock you in the hut and stand guard outside! Don't be afraid, my boy... I'll make myself scarce when she approaches, so she doesn't feel ashamed.'

And he laughed.

Andreas ran helter-skelter down the slope and the old man watched him full of hatred. 'I've talked you into it,' he said to himself. 'Now you'll leave your mark! And then I'll laugh, oh how I'll laugh!' Then he looked about. He was alone. Taking the seeds from his pouch, he mixed them with dry soil, entered the vineyard and with a mad gleam in his eye started sprinkling seed among the vines, steadily advancing down the rows. 'Next year,' he said to himself again, 'you won't harvest a single grape. The tares will have choked the vines. Not this year even, my gorse switch in the dead of night will see to that! I shall make you suffer on all fronts! Mark my word, mark my word...'

Then he turned towards the neighbour's field. The oxen were still resting beneath the olive tree, and Thomas looked at them thoughtfully a while, as if pondering the deed he had been planning, and finally he said to himself, 'Ah, no! the neighbour has never done me any harm, nor have his oxen! Enough is enough...' Tears suddenly started to his eyes and he thought about his own approaching death; his days were numbered now. He remembered his wife's terrible ordeal during her last night. And yet she had been a just and virtuous woman, no evil deeds had weighed upon her conscience, she had lived a decent life... Whereas he himself had now become a fiend... He had destroyed the fruits of people's labour, he had harmed Aglaïa's prospects by poisoning the blessed vineyard and he was hatching further evil plans. How would his wretched soul ever escape his sinful body in his final hour? But then he remembered all the persecution he had suffered, the malice he had experienced from people, and his heart hardened once again. He gazed with hatred at the doomed vineyard laden with black grapes, at the women bringing in the harvest in the valley and at Andreas trying to stay close to Amalia and tease her when he got the chance. And again he chuckled gleefully. Then he sat down beneath a tree and began to wait... and wait...

In the field below, the women were cutting the golden yellow cobs and filling up the panniers. Andreas would then empty them onto a heap under a large fig tree at the edge of the field. Now and then

Amalia would leave the harvesters to tend her sheep under the olive trees, and Andreas would follow her, on the pretext of giving her a hand, and talk to her. Neither Yannis nor Argyris were anywhere to be seen.

Finally towards midday Andreas came back up to the hut to fetch the donkey, while the women filled the sacks and fastened them. They would need to make four trips in total, all of them that same afternoon, as the village was close by.

First to set off were the brothers' wives, Chrysanthi with the laden donkey slowly leading the way, her head wobbling a little, followed by Maria and further back Aglaïa, each with a bundle of sticks balanced on her head. Amalia remained behind under the olive trees minding her sheep, while Andreas returned to sit with Thomas and guard the corn already harvested.

After a while the old man winked at him slyly and said in a low voice, 'Call her . . . Now's your chance . . . Take an old man's advice.'

Andreas heeded him and called out loudly to his cousin. She didn't dare to disobey. The two of them watched as she came up through the vineyard.

'You see, she's coming,' chuckled Thomas. 'What did I tell you? They say that if shame did not restrain them, women would behave much worse than men because their desires are more intense.* Ha, ha, ha! can't you tell, my lad, Amalia is in heat?'

The youth looked at him and the blood rushed to his face. Then he gazed with fascination at Amalia, who by now had reached them, and suddenly seizing her by the hand, drew her resolutely towards the hut. She made a show of resistance but then followed him.

Thomas laughed again and said to her, 'Don't be ashamed, my dear, I've known your little secret all along, and as you see I've never breathed a word. What would I gain by trying to spoil your fun? I'm human too and know the needs that human beings have . . . You're doing the right thing, my children, of course you are, good luck to you . . . Enjoy yourselves while you're still young; I'll be sitting here and keeping an eye out for you . . .'

His face assumed a kindly expression and he gave them a fatherly nod.

Finally the young couple disappeared into the hut. Thomas laughed aloud and getting up at once, crept over to the door and drew the sturdy wooden bolt across. Then he scrambled gleefully up to the main road and waited.

A number of people happened to be passing — women driving their flocks, men with laden horses or with hoes over their shoulders. And Thomas would stop them and, radiant with joy, announce, 'I've locked the cousins in the hut... Ha, ha, ha! Andreas and Amalia are now man and wife. Go and see for yourselves.'

'A curse upon them...' muttered several women.

'Incestuous trash...' sneered others.

The men laughed heartily, as most of them hated Argyris with a vengeance. All hurried off towards the village to be the first to spread the word.

Soon Thomas spotted Maria in the distance, descending from the village at a run, and from the way she was gesticulating he could tell that she was furious. Behind her came Yannis, corpulent as ever and evidently out of breath, as he was having difficulty keeping up with her, followed more slowly by the stooping figure of Chrysanthi, with her daughter tugging the donkey bringing up the rear.

Maria was the first to reach him and halted for a moment, her face bright red and sweating. He looked at her brazenly and started laughing.

'You scoundrel, Hangman Thomas,' she said fuming, 'it was you, you who talked them into it! You've ruined her for ever. Shame on you!' And she spat.

But the old man went on laughing without lowering his impudent gaze. Maria could restrain her rage no longer: taking off her headscarf and flinging it to the ground, she went up to Thomas, seized him by his jacket and started shaking him with all her might; then gritting her teeth, she punched him two or three times directly in the face.

'Take that, and that, you godless reprobate!' she shouted.

But Thomas offered no resistance, merely cowering a little fearfully while continuing to laugh. Maria would have gone on giving him a drubbing, but despite her fury she realized that she was wasting precious time and so turned and ran on down the hill towards the hut, cursing as she went.

'You're a dishonourable villain, Hangman Thomas!' she screamed over her shoulder.

The old man followed at a little distance, stooping low and inwardly rejoicing. He watched her draw back the bolt and enter the hut. A moment later he reached the door himself. The young couple were still locked in one another's arms, not having had time to draw apart, and trembling with fear. In a towering rage, Maria immediately hurled herself upon them, slapping, kicking, cursing and spitting at them for all she was worth.

'God damn you, you incestuous brats,' she screamed at them. 'What have you done to us, Hangman Thomas... You have scourged us without mercy!'

The young couple put up no resistance. At this point Yannis entered the hut, red-faced, perspiring and smiling as usual beneath his drooping moustache. He chuckled for a moment, looked round thoughtfully and finally said to Maria, 'Leave them alone now, to hell with them... You're only making matters worse, much worse! Just calm down, woman! Amalia has harmed no one but herself! She could have married a rich man from our village or elsewhere; now as soiled goods she'll have to marry a poor man, somebody inferior, because her market value has gone down. She's the one who'll kick herself...'

He looked at Thomas and the two men laughed.

Maria suddenly stopped beating the youngsters and glared at the men furiously. Then her anger turned to despair and her bloodshot eyes filled with tears.

'Damn it, Statiris, have you no pride!' she said to her husband, knocking her head with her fists in frustration, then flinging her headscarf to the ground she burst into tears.

Here Chrysanthi too entered the hut, pale, bent and trembling from head to foot, but a lump in her throat prevented her from crying out, and only her lips moved.

'Ah, Hangman Thomas,' she croaked, 'you've ruined our children... You're the one who put them up to it... So this is how you show us your respect...'

'You evil mummy,' Maria screamed at her, 'raising such a monster of a son...'

And she again started pummelling Andreas.

'It's all your daughter's fault, she's just like you,' Chrysanthi hissed.

Then all of them started screaming and yelling at once: the young couple as they were being mercilessly beaten, Maria frothing at the mouth with rage, Thomas gleefully mimicking the cousins' cries as the blows rained down upon them, Yannis attempting to put an end to the fracas and the neighbour with the oxen joining in; while Chrysanthi, pale and trembling, tried to intervene and shield her son, only to receive the blows herself.

Finally Argyris appeared. Tall, stout and deathly pale, he entered the hut panting for breath and sweating profusely. He immediately gave his son a hefty thwack with his stout stick and drove him from the hut.

Then, still panting and white to the lips, he said, 'So this is how you've behaved towards us, Hangman Thomas . . . I'm now obliged to expel you from my home, go to court if you want to cancel the life annuity agreement. I've nourished a serpent in my bosom and it has bitten me . . . Silence there, you women . . .'

Then he slumped to the floor as if he had just fainted. Everyone quietened down and Chrysanthi at once started fanning him with her headscarf and lamenting tearfully.

Thomas roared with laughter and set off back toward the village.

# XII

Some time had now elapsed. Maria, Amalia and Aglaïa, their pitchers on their heads, had been fetching water up from the village well since crack of dawn. In the yard, Yannis, barefoot and in shirtsleeves, his trousers rolled up to his knees, a white hankie round his neck to protect him from the sun, was tirelessly and happily mixing a pile of mortar with his hoe, spattering himself with tiny flecks of lime; while high up on the scaffold two masons were at work, one a young man in European clothes, with a torn apron and a large straw hat, his hair flaxen, his eyes vacant as a corpse's, his nose red from too much wine, the other a much older man in wide rustic breeches, a lanky fellow with a curious face that left one in doubt whether he was being serious or ironic. The younger man would shape a rough stone and, after laying a bed of mortar on the finished row, he'd drop it in and hammer it firmly into place, wedging rubble and wadding in the joints; meanwhile his mate was patiently seating the solid marble door-post, embracing it and twisting and adjusting it before checking it against the plumb-line, closing one eye to find the vertical. Andreas, stripped to the waist, was handing the building materials up to the two masons, while Argyris, pale, stout and breathing heavily, was sitting on a large stone in the middle of the site, his thick stick between his chubby legs, his restless eyes darting here and there, making sure that the work was progressing satisfactorily. Outside, Chrysanthi could be heard cooking in the kitchen.

They were rebuilding Thomas's house and the new dwelling was nearing completion.

Raising his stick, Argyris prodded the marble door-post the old mason was adjusting and with a smile remarked in his high falsetto voice, 'See you get it straight, or when the carpenters come to hang the door they'll curse you!'

'I don't need your advice,' replied the old man testily. 'Allow me to do my work as I see fit, or take the tools and build the house yourself . . . I've built I don't know how many houses and bell towers in my day, and everything I put my hand to becomes a timeless monument. My name will live on for ever!'

'We're going to run out of sand again,' shouted Yannis coughing and straightening up a moment, the hoe in both hands, his eyes half-closed 'We'll have to hire a couple of horses to bring up more tomorrow. And cartage isn't cheap.'

Just then the women returned from the well and poured water from their pitchers into the half-empty barrel. Then all three sat down on the ground together in the shade.

'I'm dripping,' exclaimed Maria, wiping her brow.

'Thomas certainly had his uses with his donkey,' remarked Argyris thoughtfully.

'Where can he have gone to?' said Maria, biting her lip. 'Perhaps we were wrong to get so upset... What if the cousins were locked inside the hut? He was the one who locked them in, and it's not as if they'd never been alone together, they're with one another day and night. Of course...'

'You overdid it,' said Argyris gravely.

'He's a queer fish, you know,' said the younger mason, hammering away at another stone. 'There's something not quite right about him... Doesn't he realise that the more he reacts like that, the worse it is? The children think it's all a game and crucify him without mercy, and he comes out with such weird remarks the adults too find him amusing; they encourage the children to bait him just for laughs! Like a show.'

'In Thomas's shoes,' Yannis remarked, 'I'd have collapsed if I could no longer vent my spleen...'*

'He even gave our Olga a good hiding,' said Maria. 'He was sitting in the doorway with a long bamboo stick hidden just inside the house. Olga approached him unsuspectingly, but he'd been watching out for her and suddenly, wham-bang! No wonder he has made himself scarce!' — Everybody laughed. — 'If there had been other children around, he'd have thrashed them too... And yet he often wept... Perhaps he felt remorse for his own malice...'

'Thomas,' said the older mason, now working on the wall, 'is an evil man... Everybody hates him... Name me one person who likes him. I'm old and a bit weird myself, but why is it that no one calls me names? By God, that tells you something!'

'He'll turn up soon enough,' said Yannis thoughtfully.

'I'll bet you,' said the younger mason, 'that by this evening or tomorrow at the latest he'll turn up like a bridegroom, mounted on his ass! Where else can he go? . . . And there'll be plenty of work awaiting him! Ha, ha, ha! Butter him up until he carts us some more sand!'

Just then Maria's two boys returned from school, clutching their dirty battered books, and came skipping into the unfinished house. They gazed proudly round the new dwelling that was taking shape, with its white doorstep and solid walls, pointing out to one another where their few sticks of furniture might fit and adding a token stone or two to the completed masonry.

'It's already lunchtime!' Argyris remarked thoughtfully. 'The day's half over! Not much work accomplished! The lintels are still not set in place.'

The masons gave him a sidelong glance. Just then Chrysanthi appeared outside the wall and quietly announced, 'Come when you like, the food is ready.'

The masons promptly left their tools on the wall where they were working and wiped their hands. The younger one looked down towards the village main-street, as he usually did, and a moment later burst out laughing and exclaimed, 'Hangman Thomas is back! Look, there he is! Well, well, well!'

'Yes, there he is,' laughed the other mason, pointing with his finger.

The three women rushed into the garden and stood together in a row, looking down with eager curiosity. And sure enough, the old man was approaching astride his tired donkey, bent, emaciated, his eyes downcast, his clothes all soiled and tattered, his thick stick in his hand and as he rode he sighed repeatedly, avoiding people's gaze.

The women laughed.

In the village a number of men were standing about or sitting outside the wine-stores, and all of them watched him curiously, with secret smiles that were on the point of erupting into laughter. The donkey slowly advanced along one side of the street, and every so often the old man would whack it or kick it in the ribs, muttering some imprecation.

Suddenly an urchin behind him started drumming on an old tin can and shouting, 'Welcome, Hangman Thomas!'

The whole village promptly burst into uproarious laughter. The old man started and flushed scarlet. He raised his head and glared at the crowd with hatred, then heaving a sigh and looking down again, he gave the beast a vicious whack and said to it, 'Get a move on there,

Argyris, God damn your father... You've brought all this upon my head, may God repay you... Giddy-up...'

The villagers laughed again, murmuring amongst themselves. The old man meanwhile rode on towards the house, muttering, 'My God, what people, what people. They'll crucify me to the very last. They've all conspired against me... It's time my life came to an end, high time... Giddy-up...'

This was greeted by another gale of laughter. And the boy again beat the tin can, shouting out once more, 'Hangman Thomas...'

The old man, who was by now making his way up the hill, did not reply but bending lower over his donkey began weeping inconsolably. Despite herself, Maria smiled and said, 'Poor thing!'

At last the old man halted under the trellis of their house, tethered his donkey and looked about him curiously. The whole place had been transformed. His old home was no more and the new building with its twin windows now stood proudly in its place. He paused irresolutely for a moment and then shook his head. Argyris now approached him grandly and greeted him with a smile on his pale lips, but the old man did not reciprocate.

'Wherever have you been, Thomas?' he asked. 'We've demolished your house and built a mansion in its place, and you weren't even here!' Then looking him over with distaste he continued gravely, 'What a state you're in — filthy, wretched and in rags... However did you get like this? Is it seemly to be going about in such disgusting clothes? Or are you doing it deliberately to shame us?'

'Yes,' he answered through clenched teeth, glaring back at him with hatred.

'But where have you been all this time?' Argyris asked again, changing the topic.

'Oh well,' sighed the old man, 'what sort of life was it anyway, here in your house... The things your children put me through — all of them, but especially Olga. Maria has poisoned my life, the annuity agreement can't be cancelled and I've become an evil man and consigned my soul to Hell! Everything belongs to you now, may none of you enjoy it... You've rebuilt my house as if I were already dead, without so much as asking me... I left and went to stay with my sister's children, but they rightly turned me from the door. They are poor but honest decent people. Whereas back here it was always

Hangman Thomas, Hangman Thomas without mercy or relief! . . . Oh, you're so unjust, the pack of you! Day and night, day and night the same! . . . So I gave my wretched donkey a good whack and off we rode. In town I tried to get admitted to the poorhouse, but they wouldn't have me either, because they claimed I wasn't destitute . . . But I wouldn't sell my donkey, as it was all I had left in the world and it didn't cause me grief . . . I went begging about town, but no one would give me anything, not a penny . . . because I'm still strong and fit enough to work. I very nearly starved to death, as did my wretched donkey . . . What was I to do! Well, here I am, back on your hands again . . . I've returned to end my life here. But my wrongs will haunt you.'

'Calm down,' Argyris interrupted him, 'come and have some food and drink and you'll feel better. You'll have a good life with us, Thomas; just behave yourself, and no one will annoy you. We demolished your house and converted it into a mansion, but it will be your home as well and you can stay here for the remainder of your days. For now, we've put your bed down in the storeroom. Come along.'

Thomas smiled ironically and followed Argyris into the unfinished building, forgetting for a moment his earlier resolve. Maria was standing at the door. He looked at her sullenly, sighed and then began to tremble. He had noticed a smile at the corner of her mouth which, annoyed with herself, she was trying to suppress, and he assumed that she too was mocking him like all the other villagers from the moment he had set foot inside the village.

'Ah, so you're back . . . and what a state you're in!' she said with malice.

'There is a God for victims of injustice too,' he replied.

She glared back at him and said, 'You expect justice, do you, Hangman Thomas, after everything you've done to me!'

He flushed crimson, heaved a sigh and gave her a hard look, but without loosing his temper said, 'Hangman Thomas, eh! Hangman Thomas again? Ah well, never mind . . . All things come to an end . . . What can I say? What can I say? . . . Oh, Maria, you've used your charms to beggar me, you've despised me and driven me to despair . . . What can I say . . .'

He started weeping bitter tears and hurried on down into the storeroom, leaving his donkey tethered to the vine and forgetting to put out its fodder. He could hear the masons upstairs having their lunch and Argyris's footsteps going across to join them. His bed was already made up for him and he stretched out with a sigh. He listened to Maria's voice talking non-stop to the masons and repeatedly referring to him by his nickname, as she tried to justify her conduct to the outside world.

At last the sun went down, but still he did not move. He had not fallen asleep however. He was conscious that the masons were knocking off and heard them entering the house for their supper; then without uttering a word he watched Amalia come stealthily into the storeroom with his meal, watched her light the candle, noticed her hesitate a moment, as if expecting him to say something before she left the room, then heard her giggling outside the door and Andreas's voice saying, 'To hell with Hangman Thomas, come and snuggle up with me; upstairs, they'll think you're waiting to collect his plate . . . they're all having supper and won't notice anything.'

Then he saw her poke her head in at the door again; he was lying wrapped up in his jacket with his hat still on. The young girl started tittering softly and the old man sighed, recollecting all their previous mockery.

Upstairs they were finishing their supper and the masons were departing. Tired out after the day's exertions, everyone was going to bed early. First the old man heard Yannis's footsteps as he began undressing, kicking off his shoes and yawning sleepily; a moment later he was in bed, and Thomas became conscious of Maria going to lie down beside him. This upset him so much he groaned aloud.

And upstairs Maria, as if she had heard him and intuited the cause of his distress, rapped on the floor with the heel of her shoe and shouted down, 'Hangman Thomas! Can you hear? I'm about to bed my manly husband. Listen to us and eat your heart out with frustration!'

He made no reply but again began weeping inconsolably, like a little child, then finally he whispered, 'I won't stand in your way! . . . Alas, alas!'

Then he got up from the bed.

# XIII

The next day, shortly after sunrise, the two masons returned to resume their work. Both were eager to get started and seemed in a cheerful mood. A light morning breeze was blowing and there was not a cloud in the sky. The women had been up since dawn and had already started topping up the water-barrel. Yannis had mixed a large amount of mortar, two hired horses had carted up a load of sand and Andreas had piled stones and tiles onto the scaffold ready for the masons. Maria's two little boys were still asleep; Chrysanthi was busy in the kitchen making coffee.

Soon the work was underway. The sound of hammering and the slopping of mortar mingled with the exchanges of the masons on the scaffold, and in due course Argyris too came lumbering into the unfinished building, stepped cautiously over the loose boards, sat down in the middle on an upturned chest and greeted everyone. Then with a smile on his pale lips he looked round at the new dwelling.

By now the women were again emptying their pitchers. Aglaïa remarked regretfully, 'Oh dear, our vine has wilted. Have you noticed, auntie?'

'Wilted?' replied Maria. 'How come? A shame to lose the grapes!'

'Wilted?' said Chrysanthi nervously, her head wobbling. 'We'd better cut it down at once before it dies; it's an ill omen when a tree withers inexplicably at home, it means one of the owners, God forbid, will die within the year. We must cut it down at once to avert the evil.'*

'How come it's wilted?' asked Argyris appearing at the door and looking vexed, as he had planted the vine himself.

'If you ask me,' said Maria thoughtfully, 'Thomas's donkey has been at it. Now what's the man done to us, curse the ill wind that brought him back! Why couldn't he have just stayed away? We're far better off without him!'

'He must have left it out all night unfed. What a shame...' said Argyris, much put out.

Andreas shinned down the ladder and dashed round the house, pinching Amalia on the way; a moment later his voice could be heard cursing as he chastised the wretched beast.

'What did I tell you?' said Maria. 'I guessed right as usual!'

'More to the point if you'd foreseen it!' remarked Yannis with a smile.

Andreas now reappeared in the yard, accompanied by the two girls, dragging the donkey by its halter and punching it in the head for good measure.

'You should see what it's done!' he said. 'It's stripped off all the bark, the vine has had it!'

'A shame about the grapes,' Maria said again. 'I was proud of them! The vine gave us a bit of shade as well! And now . . .'

'Don't beat the poor beast like that, lad,' said Yannis half closing his eyes, 'it didn't know any better. Give it an armful of hay! . . . then we might get some work out of it. Can't you see it's been ravenous all night, otherwise it wouldn't have destroyed the vine!'

'He's right,' observed Argyris, 'it needs to regain its strength; as soon as Thomas gets up we'll set them both to work. I'll send him down to fetch more sand.'

Cautiously he got to his feet and went over to the new window to inspect the vine, the leaves of which were drooping sadly.

'A shame! A real shame!' he said again.

'And do you think he'll go?' asked Yannis.

'He'll go like a lamb,' replied Maria, 'you'll see; I'll tell him to myself as soon as he gets up.'

Then swinging her pitcher onto her shoulder, she said to the two the girls, 'Let's be off then!'

And once again they set out for the well together.

For a while everybody worked away in silence. The sun was beginning to get scorching hot. The younger mason tied his hankie round his sunburned neck, remarking with a chuckle, 'Tomorrow we'll be putting on the roof. And you'll have the flag ready, won't you, Mr Statiris! Can we expect a decent tip tied in our hankies?'*

'Don't worry,' replied Argyris closing his little eyes, 'you'll be well satisfied!'

'I should hope so,' said the older mason. 'You're getting the house virtually scot free. All it's cost you is our wages, the marble and . . . What other expenses have you had?'

'And the stone, and the lime, and the sand?' replied Argyris.

'And Thomas's former dwelling?' laughed the older mason. 'Every morsel the poor fellow eats is paid for with hard labour.'

'Mortar!' shouted the other mason, banging with his trowel on the plank. 'Don't delay us or we won't get the roof on by tomorrow!'

Andreas climbed the ladder, a large tile heaped with mortar balanced on his shoulder, and when he reached the scaffold tipped it onto a board beside the mason.

Chrysanthi, her head wobbling, gazed round admiringly at the new building. Then she looked with equal admiration at Argyris, who had resumed his seat in the middle on the chest, and asked him, 'The new part will be ours, won't it, Argyris? It will bring us luck and I prefer it to the old one.'

Argyris gave her a wry look. 'If Maria hears you,' he scolded her, 'we'll never hear the end of it!'

The masons laughed and muttered something to each other.

Yannis answered her good-naturedly, 'What does it matter who has what, aren't they pretty much the same?'

They all continued working zealously for quite some time, as if in a hurry to complete the house that day. Yannis busily mixed the mortar with his hoe, the masons shaped the stones and set them in the wall, their hammering resounding rhythmically, and Andreas went up and down the ladder tirelessly delivering his load.

Soon the women returned from the well again and emptied their pitchers into the barrel. Chrysanthi handed them each a slice of bread and they sat down quietly in the shade to rest. They were on the point of setting off once more, still munching their bread, when Argyris appeared in the newly finished doorway and looked at them.

'And Thomas,' Maria asked him, 'still no sign of him?'

'What d'you want him for?' the younger mason asked her laughing.

'I'm in love with him!' she answered blushing scarlet, but taking no offence. 'What do I want him for? Haven't you seen my vine? It's in a woeful state ... Am I supposed to let him get away with that?'

'Not now!' Argyris told her. 'Leave him alone, for God's sake, or he might take off again and people blame us!'

'How come he isn't up yet?' Yannis asked.

'He'll be stiff from riding all day yesterday,' observed the older mason. 'Who knows how long he's been on the road!'

'Amalia, go and peep in at his door,' Argyris told her. 'Perhaps he doesn't want to leave the house because people are about and he's afraid they might start heckling him again . . . Or could he have noticed that the vine has wilted?'

Amalia got up, cursing under her breath, and went slowly out.

'How tiresome he's become,' remarked Maria with disgust.

'It's we who've made him what he is,' said Yannis.

They were now waiting for Amalia to return. Suddenly they heard a piercing scream.

'What's the matter?' cried Maria. 'I'm coming, I'm coming! The miscreant must have attacked her!'

And she dashed off to the rescue. Chrysanthi began to whimper fearfully and drew closer to Argyris, who himself went very pale; Yannis stopped what he was doing; and Andreas leaped down from the scaffold and rushed to join his cousin. But by this time she had already reappeared, pale and terrified, still screaming and biting the hem of her headscarf.

'What did he do to you, the scoundrel?' asked Maria anxiously.

But she couldn't answer. Aglaïa took both her hands and Andreas, badly shaken, asked her, 'Did he try to grab you?'

'Thomas . . . Thomas . . . Thomas . . .' screamed Amalia.

'I'll have his head, like John the Baptist,' cried Maria fuming.

'Thomas has hanged himself . . .' Amalia blurted out at last. They all looked at one another.

'Are you sure?' said Argyris, going even paler.

'Oh, how frightful,' said Maria.

'Are you sure?' said Yannis, his sleepy eyes for once wide open.

'Yes,' said Amalia, 'the door was ajar and he's hanging from a beam behind it and it spooked me! . . .'

The two masons leaped from the scaffold, Argyris stepped out through the newly finished doorway, they all looked at one another again, then everyone trooped out after Argyris. A moment later they were assembled underneath the withered vine. Amalia had left the storeroom door open and they all caught sight of him at once. He was hanging by the neck with his head to one side, as the noose had slipped and drawn tight beside his ear. His glazed, now sightless eyes were open and protruding from their hollow sockets, his tongue was lolling out, his gaping mouth left his ugly teeth exposed and his sad face was reddish-black. Hanging there motionless, his whole body somehow looked longer, now that death had stretched it, his big toes just touching the ground; while scattered about his feet where a few bricks which he had evidently piled up to get his neck into the noose and then kicked away. For a moment no one spoke and they all just stood there staring at him.

At last Maria, biting her lip and shaking her head, looked up at him angrily and said, 'Why did he choose this wicked way to go, confound him!'

The two masons burst out laughing. 'The Tempter got the better of him!' said the older one.

Argyris however seemed greatly agitated and was having difficulty breathing.

'What's he done to us!' he wheezed dejectedly. 'There'll be an uproar in the village.'

'But it's not your fault!' the other mason said dismissively. 'The Church will excommunicate him. He's usurped the hand of God, and that no man has the right to do.'

'I feel sorry for him,' Yannis sighed, 'but it's too late now. There's nothing we can do!'

'You see,' Chrysanthi moaned, 'you see what he has done to us! Now he'll come back to haunt us all at night!'

Andreas, grinning, nudged the corpse, making it sway. The movement struck him as so eerie that he laughed aloud; then he said, 'He shat himself.'

'He's as black as the Devil himself!' whispered Amalia fearfully and giggled.

'What a gruesome end to Hangman Thomas,' laughed Aglaïa nervously.

'And now he'll come back to haunt us all at night,'* wailed Chrysanthi trembling. 'We won't even be able to go out.'

'Good riddance to him!' said Maria. 'We're baptized Christians, aren't we, so all we have to do is cross ourselves and whatever might appear before our eyes will vanish instantly! Good riddance to him!'

And she gestured obscenely at the dead man with both hands.

'Fetch the ladder and we'll take him down,' said the older mason.

Andreas was about to get the ladder, but Argyris stopped him.

'Don't touch him before the authorities arrive!'

'Someone should summon them at once,' observed the mason, 'otherwise how are you going to dispose of the old spook?'

Maria's two little boys now came down and, clinging to their mother, gazed at the hanged man curiously, not quite understanding.

'Why did he hang himself?' asked one.

'Because he got tired of having to put up with us,' replied his older brother laughing.

'Off to school now!' their mother told them earnestly. But they didn't move.

Soon the whole neighbourhood had gathered. The younger mason who had gone to inform the authorities had spread the news everywhere he went, laughing as he described Thomas's demise. So now everyone was there: the girls and the old crone who had teased him on their way down to the well, the children who had beaten their tin cans as he rode through the village on his donkey, or hooted his nickname from the ridge-tops, the men who had amused themselves watching him get angry, and not a single face bore any marks of sorrow.

'What happened, Hangman Thomas, you poor wretch,' the swarthy lass was saying.

'What a grizzly end!' said the old crone in the torn man's jacket.

'Shame on you!' said the little woman with the pretty face. 'You wanted to molest us girls and bound yourself to the Devil hand and foot. Shame, I spit on you!'

'Did you see him? Did you see him?' others cried.

Suddenly several people all spat at once, while others exclaimed, 'Curse you, Hangman Thomas, curse you!'

The village children giggled and chimed in, 'Boo, boo! Hangman Thomas, boo, Hangman Thomas.'

At this, Maria's two little boys also burst out laughing.

Now the tall stout figure of the village police sergeant appeared among the crowd. He too was in a jovial mood. The onlookers made way for him to inspect the corpse. He looked at it casually, twirling a fine metal chain around his finger.

'Alright, alright,' he said a minute later, 'take him down, the doctor will examine him inside the church!'

'Inside the church,' exclaimed the older mason, 'this spook inside the church? Why don't they just chuck him straight into his grave...'

'You'll want him buried in the cemetery, no doubt...' said the sergeant.

'Not with the rest of our deceased,' said the same mason. 'Sixty paces from the nearest gravestone is what church law decrees.'

'Right then, that's where the doctor will attend,' declared the sergeant.

Meanwhile Andreas had brought the ladder round from the new building and propped it against the lintel on the inside of the storeroom. The younger mason climbed up several rungs and endeavoured to untie the knot, but without success, as the weight of the corpse held the rope taut and the soap made it slip through his hands. Realising after a while that his efforts were in vain, he shouted, 'Even now you're causing trouble, Hangman Thomas! Bring me a knife and we'll cut him down!'

Andreas immediately handed him a knife and he set about severing the rope, which soon snapped. Suddenly the full weight of Thomas's body was taken by his legs, and for a moment he stood there upright, as if he had come to life again; then he fell heavily onto his back, hitting the ground with a thud, so that the air still trapped inside his chest escaped through his mouth as the rope gave way, making the corpse groan as if still alive.

'Did you hear him howl!' exclaimed the old crone in the torn man's jacket, crossing herself.

For a moment the crowd fell silent, suddenly afraid, then everybody laughed and the children squeezed past the women to see the outstretched corpse and again began to chant, 'Boo, boo! Hangman Thomas!'

'Be gone with you,' said Chrysanthi, her head wobbling as if to exorcise the corpse, 'and may no evil spook appear, and if it does may we not fear it!'

Four men in bare feet, their breeches rolled up to their knees, their hair unkempt, their faces stubbly, and wearing neither coats and ties nor hats, hurried in carrying the bier and laughing amongst themselves. They were the same men who had once borne Thomas's own wife. In less than a minute they had laid the corpse out on the bier, hoisted it onto their shoulders, manoeuvred it out through the door and set off down the hill at a run. No one followed, everybody just stood there watching from the yard. The severed rope was still dangling from Thomas's neck. The children dashed through the gardens and hurtled down the hillside to intercept the corpse in the main-street.

The bearers meanwhile continued running on down the hill.

Outside the stores, which were still open, the villagers had lined the street; some looked on indifferently, others cursed him, others spat as he passed by, and someone contemptuously chanted the words called out after Jewish corpses,* which likewise are run out of town: 'Run, rabbit, run, the Devil has a gun . . .'*

At this the four bearers redoubled their steps and the children beat their tin cans, as they had when he was still alive, and shouted after him, 'Boo, boo, Hangman Thomas! Boo, Hangman Thomas!'

As the corpse was passing the church in the middle of the village, Yannis's brother-in-law, the priest, happened to be outside, but even he refused his blessing and turning his impressive face away said haughtily, 'God forgive thee according to thy deeds . . .'

The children, now running along behind, continued shouting: 'Boo, boo, Hangman Thomas!' Some even tugged at the slippery rope trailing from his neck!

And so the pitiful cortège left the village and at last reached the cemetery, a large uneven patch of waste land overgrown with thistles and dry weeds on a little hill not far from the last houses.

There were very few tombstones, or even simple crosses, among the innumerable unmarked graves. A small newly built chapel with no belfry stood in the middle of the cemetery, which was without boundary walls. On arriving with the corpse, the four men placed the bier in the sun and immediately set about digging the grave, well away from the chapel in a remote spot at the foot of the hill.

Then the village doctor and the sergeant arrived, followed closely by the old notary, stooping, frail and emaciated and leaning on his stout stick, his eternal involuntary smile on his red lips.

The doctor approached the corpse, bent over it, undid the shirt and double-breasted waistcoat, took a perfunctory look and shrugged his shoulders with indifference. He was about to leave when the sergeant retrieved a small package from the dead man's waistcoat, carefully unfolded it and inside discovered two twenty-five drachma notes.

'They're for me,' exclaimed the doctor with delight.

'The gravediggers will have to be paid with one of them!' cautioned the policeman.

'So Thomas did have money after all,' said one of the young bearers. 'And yet he went and hanged himself!'

'Don't you see?' said another knowingly. 'Argyris planted those notes on him, so he couldn't be accused of having sucked him dry. Look how crisp and new they are!'

Just then the old notary came up to them, and still smiling his involuntary smile cried out in his frail voice, 'Doctor, doctor, so help me God, Argyris was the one who hanged him! Yes, Argyris, God damn his father, to get at his inheritance . . . He planned it all from the beginning, he was the one. He made a cuckold of his own brother, my son-in-law Yannis, after Thomas tupped my daughter, I know it for a fact, and Argyris arranged it all to get at his inheritance. They've done the same to me! They came to an arrangement with my son-in-law the priest, confound him, and they've put me on the street, and now I, a man of property, have to go begging! I pray to God that not a soul in that family survives, that my grandchildren perish one and all! It's true, I tell you, Argyris was the one who hanged him!'

The doctor, the policeman and the gravediggers all split their sides laughing. The grave was now ready. Just then an old woman approached the corpse, sat down beside it for a moment and said tearfully, 'Poor Thomas, you've forfeited your life and your immortal soul. What have they done to you, poor Thomas! . . .'

And she sighed; it was his sister.

Now two of the gravediggers seized hold of the dead man and brought him over to the grave, into which their comrades had already climbed, and together the four of them lowered the corpse in.

Then the notary said in his faint voice, smiling the whole time, 'Pile the earth high, then his ghost can't come back to haunt us! Bury him deep, deep!'

And as the gravediggers hastily shovelled the earth into the grave, one of them replied, 'The churchwardens want the cemetery tidying and Argyris, who is one of them, promised we would get the job, so we'll heap all the soil we shift on top of him. In two or three days no one will ever know where he's been buried! . . .'

# NOTES

These notes correspond to asterisks in the text. The heading for each note consists of the extract from the text to which the note refers, preceded by the page number. Full details of works referred to will be found in the Bibliography.

**4. he had grown so accustomed to the nickname that he no longer took offence.** A sensitive issue in traditional Mediterranean cultures, nicknaming served both as a means of identifying someone, for instance by their trade, place of origin or some personal attribute, and as a mark of social distinction or opprobrium. In the last case, using someone's nickname to their face would be highly offensive. See Pitt-Rivers, 'Honour and social status', 40.

**5. The priest intends to arrange for his son to marry soon, as he wants him to become a priest as well.** In the Orthodox Church a man intending to become a priest must either marry before he is ordained or remain celibate.

**6. he flicked his tooth with his fingernail.**
Descriptions of such gestures, many of them still in common use, are one of the hallmarks of Theotokis's village fiction and serve both a dramatic and an ethnographic function.

**6. just to catch consumption?**
The scourge of tuberculosis was widely feared and, like deformity or loss of virginity, it constituted legitimate grounds for breaking off a marital engagement.

**11. Remember what you got up to with your cousin?**
The taboo subject of incest is tackled more than once in Theotokis's village fiction, and the physical effects of inbreeding are also sometimes hinted at, for instance in the unusually wide mouth and large teeth of Argyris's son, or the small lipless mouth of the murderous Koukouliotis in 'Face down'. Luis Buñuel's early documentary *Las Hurdes*, which records the appalling squalor in a remote Spanish village in 1929, suggests that conditions like cretinism might not have been uncommon.

**12. whenever the wives started quarrelling you'd beat mine and I'd beat yours!** In such patriarchal peasant communities, wife-beating was regarded as legitimate, though considered dishonourable if carried to excess.

**14. if we split up, we'd have to take on outside labour, so we'd be feeding and paying wages to outsiders.** This illustrates the centrality of the family and its tendency to regard non-members as outsiders, and summarizes the economic benefits of extended families, better able to pool resources. In the matter of property ownership and inheritance, however, relatives by marriage were themselves regarded as outsiders, the comic potential of which Theotokis exploits to the full.

### 15. giggling surreptitiously and looking into one another's eyes.
A classic field study of the transhumant Sarakatsan shepherds of Epirus opposite Corfu describes how the segregation of the sexes outside the extended family often resulted in a close relationship between male and female cousins during adolescence, involving 'a good deal of mutual teasing [. . .] playful wrestling, bottom smacking, and cheek pinching' (Campbell, *Honour, Family, and Patronage*, 101).

### 16. And don't forget your sewing
Preparation of the dowry was a joint enterprise between mothers and their daughters, who would spend long hours embroidering for their trousseaux.

### 17. But sometimes the donkey and his master disagree.
In line with his conviction that demotic Greek should be accepted as the norm, Theotokis jotted down proverbs and idioms he heard among the peasants and used them frequently to spice up the dialogue in his fiction.

### 18. *tsarouchia* with no pompoms on his feet
Thomas's dress approximates the traditional island costume worn by men as described by Lawrence Durrell in 1945 — though by then 'seldom seen except at festivals and dances.
    Blue embroidered bolero jacket with black and gold braid and piping
    A white soft shirt with puffed sleeves
    Baggy blue breeches called Vrakes
    White woollen gaiters
    And pointed Turkish slippers with no pompom
    Either a soft, red fez with a blue tassel
    Or a white straw hat' (*Prospero's Cell*, 10).

### 21. They say there was a rod in paradise, yes, slap in the middle.
Hence the widespread saying that 'the rod derived from Paradise' (*to xylo vyike ap' ton paradeiso*).

### 21. And men should never get splenetic [...] Anger is quite different
Thomas's distinction is remotely based on Galen's physiology of the four humours, which were held to influence temperament. A predominance of blood produced sanguine types, of phlegm phlegmatic types, of yellow bile choleric types, and of black bile melancholic types. The spleen was regarded as the seat of melancholy, or morose feelings.

# NOTES

**22. St Spyridon**
The patron saint and protector of Corfu against Turkish invasions and natural disasters, whose preserved body is kept in the Italianate church named after him and is paraded round the town on at least three occasions each year.

**27. nephews and nieces are never quite the same.**
According to another popular saying, 'to whom God does not give children, the Devil gives nephews and nieces' (*s' opion den dinei o theos paidia, dinei o diavolos anipsia*).

**28. A cock crowed once, twice, three times and then fell silent.**
A cock crowing was thought to be a harbinger of death, a tradition related to Christ's words to Peter on the Mount of Olives: 'this night, before the cock crow, thou shalt deny me thrice' (Matthew 26.34).

**29. I spit on him!**
As well as an expression of contempt, (metaphoric) spitting was a common form of exorcism, as in the expression *Phtou na mi baskatheis* ('Spit, that you may be safe from the evil eye').

**32. Her heirs will be upon us soon and they'll take anything that belonged to her...** If there were no male children in a marriage, it was customary when the wife died for the property she brought with her by way of dowry to revert to her own family.

**33. Haven't we met somewhere before?**
It was popularly believed that souls were like air and neither married couples nor immediate family members would recognize each other after death, beyond a dim sense of familiarity.

**34. Suddenly in the garden his donkey started braying.**
In some parts of Greece, the donkey was associated with the Devil and its braying before dawn was considered ominous.

**39. Where do apples fall? Underneath the apple tree...**
The saying that 'the apple will fall under the apple tree' (*to milo apokat' ap' ti milia tha pesi*) was also current among the Sarakatsan shepherds and refers to the belief that evil people come from evil stock and beget evil progeny.

**39–40. four young men smartly dressed in European clothes**
The Greek term is *phrangika roucha* meaning 'Frankish clothes'. Frankish is not specifically 'French' but refers to western Europeans generally.

**40. the priests' brightly coloured vestments, all turned inside out**
Perhaps a significant detail, as garments were often worn inside out or back to front to ward off spells or evil spirits.

# NOTES

**43. Beautiful a beauty is, five or ten times over / But best of all's a woman with her lover.** Theotokis shared the interest in traditional folksong of his time and would jot down songs he heard in taverns or at village weddings and festivities to use in his fiction. In his story 'Reputation', two rivals for a young squire's affections sing this kind of improvised rhyming couplet (*mantinada*) in a musical exchange of insults. Lawrence Durrell reports (*Prospero's Cell*, 111) that one of his Greek friends was struck by the poetic beauty of a professional mourner's spontaneous oral laments.

**47. a sweet fiver**
The Greek term *talaro* (derived like 'dollar' from German 'Taler') was commonly used in Theotokis' time to refer to a silver five-drachma coin — a generous day's wage for a villager.

**52. signed his soul over to the Devil, keeping nothing but a teaspoon in his sash.** Spoons were sometimes used in exorcising rituals, for instance by mothers whose children had been given the evil eye and fallen sick. The English proverb, 'he who would sup with the Devil should go with a long spoon', has lost any superstitious overtones it may once have had.

**52. he's a regular wild boar!**
Like the goat, the boar was regarded both as a symbol of potency and as one of the Devil's protean manifestations, others, besides the donkey, being the black dog and the hare.

**54. they're so jealous she often gets the evil eye**
The evil eye, closely associated with envy, the Devil's sin, was a major preoccupation in the folk psyche of the time, and all manner of phylacteries and charms were used against it.

**55. Argyris, long may he live, is the helmsman of this household.**
A succinct recent summary of the Greek patriarchal system explains that, 'a man of honour or *timi*' was expected to 'demonstrate at all times a firm command over all things that matter in the lives of Greek peasant men: land, property, animals and the people in his household [...] himself [included]. Exercising control of resources defined his role as *nikokyris* (literally, lord of the household).' He 'was to use every means at his disposal, deception, prevarication, intimidation and even violence to defend the social standing and enhance the material welfare of his household [...] He was to ensure harmony within it as well. Calling into question a woman's sexual reputation cut so deep in this culture because it struck at the heart of masculinity: a man's ability to control the most important element in his household — his wife's or his daughter's reproductive behaviour' (Gallant, *Modern Greece*, 101-3).

# NOTES

**58. clean-shaven, in new *tsarouchia* and straw hat.**
At weddings traditionally the groom would appear freshly shaven and in a new suit of clothes. Sometimes the bride would ride through the village on a donkey, whereas once married her place would be on foot behind her mounted lord and master.

**62. hugger-mugger like the gypsies ...**
The gypsies on Corfu, valued during Venetian times for their horse-breeding skills, were looked down on by the common people who regarded them as shameless.

**63. my father made us all notaries like himself [...] thanks to the British and the old nobility.** Local notaries would have been in higher demand during the Protectorate than after the Union with Greece, when governance of the islands was transferred to Athens.

**68. What guarantees would you have with an undertaking from a married woman?** In Greece it was not until the 1980s, under the moderate socialist government of Andreas Papandreou, that legislation was passed releasing women from the absolute control of their husbands, abolishing the dowry system, legalizing civil marriage, decriminalizing adultery and simplifying divorce procedures.

**77. I'm the one who's caught you in a sack**
There are suggestive parallels between Thomas's fate and that of the lustful Falstaff caught in a basket and pinched and pummelled by children around Herne the hunter's haunted oak in Shakespeare's *The Merry Wives of Windsor* and Verdi's *Falstaff*, though the midsummer mood and happy endings of these works could not be more different.

**82. To avoid setting the churches, which are Orthodox, on fire as well.**
While there were Jewish and Catholic (mainly Maltese rather than Italian) minorities in Corfu Town, each with its place of worship, the village churches were Greek Orthodox.

**89. and the crosses stand there as a warning to this day.**
Thomas's hate-filled anecdote sums up both the cruelty and the misogyny of the age. Hanging was used in the islands under the British, and hanging, drawing and quartering (of men) for treason was not formally abolished in Britain until 1871. Decapitation was more common under the Ottomans, but Byron on his visit to the Albanian Ali Pasha of Ioannina was confronted by gruesome evidence of quartering. The way the restricted lives of village women could lead to madness is powerfully dramatized in Papadiamandis's novella, *The murderess*.

## NOTES

### 91. just like John the Baptist.
The story of Salome dancing before Herod and demanding John the Baptist's head as a reward, popular among fin-de-siècle artists, is alluded to again later, inviting comparison between Salome's conduct and that of Maria herself.

### 95. I'll become a fiend!
The Greek word *Peirasmos* is richer in the context than 'fiend', meaning 'temptation' and by extension the 'Tempter', or the Devil.

### 98. It will be worse than a hailstorm striking!
The Sarakatsan shepherds of Epirus believed that 'high winds, storms, whirl-winds, are manifestations of demonic power' (Campbell, 'Honour and the Devil', 160).

### 100. Is her father going to kill you, are her little brothers?
According to the prevailing code of honour, such matters were a stain on the whole family and the duty of vengeance extended to brothers and even cousins. Blood feuds could extend for generations, as notoriously in neighbouring Albania, and wipe out whole families.

### 103. women would behave much worse than men because their desires are more intense.
A widespread and deeply held belief, underpinned by Judeo-Christian myth and doctrine and central to various codes of honour throughout the Mediterranean and Near East.

### 108. I'd have collapsed if I could no longer vent my spleen . . .
The Greek *gremistei*, meaning 'collapsed', puns playfully on *kremastei*, meaning 'hanged myself', without giving the game away.

### 113. We must cut it down at once to avert the evil.
The belief in magical transference of this kind was widespread. In Epirus for instance a sick child's bedding was spread out for the hens to walk on and assume the illness. Elsewhere, when sheep or cattle were afflicted, a piglet would be tarred, set alight and made to run among the herd to take the disease upon itself.

### 114. Can we expect a decent tip tied in our hankies?
Traditionally gifts were wrapped in hankies, particularly at weddings, where even today sugared almonds are presented to the guests tied in little bundles.

### 117. He shat himself [...] he'll come back to haunt us all at night
In popular belief, the soul of the suicide 'instead of departing through the mouth (as some imagine it in the form of a small bird) and rising to God [...] passes through the anus to the Devil'. The body 'remains undissolved in the earth and possessed by the spirit of the Devil emerges from its grave' at night to haunt and terrify the living (Campbell, 'Honour and the Devil', 164).

# NOTES

**120. chanted the words called out after Jewish corpses**
It was believed that Judas's descendants had settled in Corfu, and the still-practiced custom of throwing old crockery down into the street at Easter has been interpreted as his ritual stoning. Jews in Venetian times were liable to be press-ganged into galleys, employed as porters and even used as executioners, but during the nineteenth century they came to play an increasing role in the Island's finances (see Potts, 'The Jewish communities'). In his novel *Slaves in their chains*, anti-semitism among the Corfiot aristocracy is one of Theotokis's satiric targets.

**120. Run, rabbit, run, the Devil has a gun . . .**
This conveys the incantatory quality of the Greek, *lagos, lagos tou diavolou kinigos* (literally: 'hare, hare, the Devil's hunter'), but not the notion that the hare is itself a manifestation of the devil.

# BIBLIOGRAPHY

**Theotokis: works**

Θεοτόκης, Κωνταντίνος (Konstantinos Theotokis), *Η ζωή και ο θάνατος του Καραβέλα* (*The life and death of Karavelas* [the hangman]), ed. Spyros Kokkinis. Athens: Estia, 1990; 1st edn 1920.

———, *Η τιμή και το χρήμα* (*Honour and cash*). Athens: Pagoulatos, 2007; 1st edn 1912.

———, *Ἡ χάση τοῦ κόσμου – Τὸ ὄνειρο τοῦ Σάτνη – Κέρκυρα: ἀνέκδοτα διηγήματα* (*Waning of the world – Satni's dream – Kerkyra: unpublished stories*). Athens: Keimena, 1981.

———, *Κορφιάτικες ιστορίες* (*Corfiot tales*). Athens: Gavriilidis, 2005; 1st edn 1935.

———, *Ο κατάδικος* (*The Convict*). Athens: Kalokathis, 2001; 1st edn 1919.

———, *Οι σκλάβοι στα δεσμά τους* (*Slaves in their chains*). Athens: Synchroni Epochi, 2007; 1st edn 1922.

Théotoki, Constantin, *Le condamné*, tr. Léon Krajewski. Paris: Calmann-Lévy, 1929.

Théotokis, Constantin, *L'honneur et l'argent*, tr. Lucile Farnoux. Paris: Cambourakis, 2015; 1st edn 1996.

Theotokis, Konstantinos, *Slaves in their chains*, tr. J. M. Q. Davies. London: Angel Classics, 2014.

Théotoky, Cte C., *Vie de Montagne*. Paris: Perrin, 1895.

**Theotokis: biographical and critical material**

Δάλλας, Γιάννης (Yannis Dallas), *Κωνσταντίνος Θεοτόκης: κριτική σπουδή μιας πεζογραφικής πορείας* (*Konstantinos Theotokis: a critical study of his career as a prose writer*). Athens: Ekdoseis Sokoli, 2001.

Θεοτόκης, Σπυρίδων Μ. (Spyridon M. Theokokis), *Τα νεανικά χρόνια του Κωνσταντίνου Θεοτόκη: βιογραφία* (*The early years of Konstantinos Theotokis: a biography*), ed. Tasos Korphis. Athens: Prosperos, 1983.

Φιλίππου, Φίλιππος (Philippos Philippou), *Κωνσταντίνος Θεοτόκης: σκλάβος του πάθους* (*Konstantinos Theotokis: slave to passion*). Athens: Electra, 2006.

Χουρμούζιος, Αιμίλιος (Emilios Chourmouzios), *Κωνσταντίνος Θεοτόκης: ο εισηγητής του κοινωνιστικού μυθιστορήματος στην Ελλάδα* (*Konstantinos Theotokis: the founder of the social novel into Greece*). Athens: Ekdoseis ton Philon, 1979.

Davies, J. M. Q., 'Konstantinos Theotokis and Giuseppe di Lampedusa: literary responses to turbulent times', in Hirst and Sammon, *The Ionian Islands*, 385–93.

Dermitzakis, Babis, 'Honor and shame in the work of Constantinos Theotokis', *Canadian Review of Comparative Literature* 25.3 (1988), 554–61.

**Related literary works**

Durrell, Gerald, *The Corfu Trilogy*. London: Penguin, 2006). Includes *My family and other animals* (1956), *Birds, beasts and relatives* (1969), and *The Garden of the Gods* (1979).

Durrell, Lawrence, *Prospero's Cell: a guide to the landscape and manners of the island of Corcyra*. London: Faber & Faber, 2000; 1st edn 1945.

Karkavitsas, Andreas, *The beggar*, tr. W. F. Wyatt. New York: Caratzas, 1982.

Kazantzakis, Nikos, *Christ recrucified: a novel*, tr. Jonathan Griffin. Oxford: B. Cassirer, 1954.

———, *Freedom and death*, tr. Johathan Griffin. London: Faber & Faber, 1966.

Lampedusa, Giuseppe Tomassi di, *The Leopard*, tr. Archibald Colquhoun. London: Vintage, 2007 (revised edn); 1st edn 1961.

Lear, Edward *The Corfu years*, ed. Philip Sherrard. Athens & Dedham: Denise Harvey, 1988.

Myrivilis, Stratis, *Life in the tomb*, tr. Peter Bien. Hanover, NH: University Press of New England, 1977.

———, *The mermaid madonna*, tr. Abbot Rick. Athens: Efstathiadis, 1981

———, *The schoolmistress with the golden eyes*, tr. Philip Sherrard. London: Hutchinson, 1964.

Papadiamandis, Alexandros, *Around the lagoon: reminiscences to a friend*, tr. Peter Mackridge. Limni, Evia: Denise Harvey, 2014.

———, *Tales from a Greek island*, tr. Elizabeth Constantinidies. Baltimore, MD: The Johns Hopkins University Press, 1987.

———, *The murderess: a social tale*, tr. Liadain Sherrard. Limni, Evia: Denise Harvey, 2011.

Verga, Giovanni, *Cavalleria Rusticana and other stories*, tr. G. H. McWilliam. London: Penguin, 1999.

———, *I Malavoglia: The house by the medlar tree*, tr. Judith Landy. Sawtry: Dedalus, 1985.

Vizyenos, Georgios, *My mother's sin and other stories*, tr. William F. Wyatt, Jr. Hanover, NH: University Press of New England, 1988.

**Historical and cultural background**

Beaton, Roderick, *Folk poetry of modern Greece*. Cambridge: Cambridge University Press, 1980.

——— (ed.), *The Greek novel A.D. 1–1985*. London: Croom Helm, 1988.

# BIBLIOGRAPHY

Campbell, J. K., 'Honour and the Devil', in Peristiany, *Honour and shame*.
———, *Honour, family and patronage: a study of institutions and moral values in a Greek mountain community*. Oxford: Clarendon Press, 1964.
Crawley, Roger, *City of fortune: how Venice won and lost a naval empire* (London: Faber & Faber, 2011).
Dakin, Douglas, *The unification of Greece 1770-1923*. London: Ernest Benn, 1972.
Flamburiari, Spiro L., *Corfu: the garden isle*. London: John Murray, 1994.
Fleming, K. E., *The Muslim Bonaparte: diplomacy and orientalism in Ali Pasha's Greece*. Princeton: Princeton University Press, 1999.
Gallant, Thomas W., *Modern Greece*. London: Hodder Arnold, 2001.
Gilmore, David D., *Honor and shame and the unity of the Mediterranean*. Arlington, VA: American Anthropological Association, 1987.
Herzfeld, Michael, *The Poetics of manhood: contest and identity in a Cretan mountain village*. Princeton: Princeton University Press, 1985.
Hirst, Anthony and Patrick Sammon (eds), *The Ionian Islands: aspects of their history and culture*. Newcastle upon Tyne: Cambridge Scholars Publishing, 2014.
Holland, Robert *Blue-water empire: the British in the Mediterranean since 1800*. London: Penguin, 2013.
Jervis, Henry Jervis White, *History of the Island of Corfu and of the Republic of the Ionian Islands*. Amsterdam: B. R. Grüner, 1970 (reprint); 1st edn 1852.
Mackridge, Peter, *Language and national identity in Greece 1776–1976*. Oxford: Oxford University Press, 2009.
———, 'Venise apres Venise: offical languages in the Ionian Islands, 1797–1864', *Byzantine and Modern Greek Studies* 38.1 (2014), 68–90.
Megas, Georgios, ed., *Folk tales of Greece*, tr. Helen Colaclides. Chicago: University of Chicago Press, 1970.
Myrsiades, Linda S., *Karagiozis: culture and comedy in Greek puppet theatre*. Lexington: University of Kentucky Press, 1992.
Peristiany, J. G. (ed.), *Honour and shame: the values of Mediterranean society*. Chicago: University of Chicago Press, 1966.
Pitt-Rivers, Julian, 'Honour and social status', in Peristiany, *Honour and shame*.
Politis, Linos, *A history of modern Greek literature*. Oxford: Clarendon Press, 1973.
Potts, Jim, 'The fate of the Jewish communities of Corfu, Zakynthos and Ioannina', in Hirst and Sammon, *The Ionian Islands*, 221–230.
———, *The Ionian Islands and Epirus: a cultural history*. Oxford: Signal Books, 2010.
Pratt, Michael, *Britain's Greek empire*. London: Rex Collings, 1978.
St Clair, William, *That Greece might still be free: the Philhellenes in the War of Independence*. London: Oxford University Press, 1972.
Stewart, Charles, *Demons and the Devil: moral imagination in modern Greek culture*. Princeton: Princeton University Press, 1991.
Young, Martin, *Corfu and the other Ionian Islands* (London: Jonathan Cape, 1971).